D0113999

OH, RATS!

Also by Tor Seidler

Firstborn

Mean Margaret

The Wainscott Weasel

OH, RATS!

Tor Seidler

Illustrated by Gabriel Evans

A Caitlyn Dlouhy Book

A ATHENEUM BOOKS FOR YOUNG READERS
atheneum   New York   London   Toronto   Sydney   New Delhi

ATHENEUM BOOKS FOR YOUNG READERS

An imprint of Simon & Schuster Children's Publishing Division

1230 Avenue of the Americas, New York, New York 10020

ATHENEUM BOOKS FOR YOUNG READERS is a registered trademark of Simon & Schuster, Inc. Atheneum logo is a trademark of Simon & Schuster, Inc.

For information about special discounts for bulk purchases, please contact Simon & Schuster Special Sales at 1-866-506-1949 or business@simonandschuster.com.

The Simon & Schuster Speakers Bureau can bring authors to your live event. For more information or to book an event, contact the Simon & Schuster Speakers Bureau at 1-866-248-3049 or visit our website at www.simonspeakers.com.

Book design by Greg Stadnyk and Karyn Lee

The text for this book was set in Garamond.

The illustrations for this book were rendered in pencil and gouache.

Manufactured in the United States of America

0719 FFG • First Edition

2 4 6 8 10 9 7 5 3 1

Library of Congress Cataloging-in-Publication Data

Names: Seidler, Tor, author. | Evans, Gabriel, illustrator.

Title: Phoenix / Tor Seidler ; illustrated by Gabriel Evans.

Description: First edition. | New York : Atheneum, [2019] | "A Caitlyn Dlouhy Book." | Summary: "A New Jersey squirrel named Phoenix teams up with a pack of rats in New York City to save their riverside home from being demolished and turned into a high-rise"—Provided by publisher.

Identifiers: LCCN 2018045417| ISBN 9781534426849 (hardcover) | ISBN 9781534426863 (eBook)

Subjects: | CYAC: Adventure and adventurers—Fiction. | Squirrels—Fiction. | Rats—Fiction. | New York (N.Y.)—Fiction.

Classification: LCC PZ7.S45526 Pho 2019 | DDC [Fic]—dc23

LC record available at https://lccn.loc.gov/2018045417

For Annabel

1

PURPLE BERRIES

PHOENIX WOKE UP EARLY AND DECIDED TO GO LOOK for some food. He'd actually never ventured out of the nest, which was in a hole about a third of the way up a pine tree, but he *had* poked his head out to watch his parents go foraging. They descended the tree headfirst, so he assumed this was how it was done. But when he got out onto the bark and turned that way, he started trembling, and his left whiskers twitched uncontrollably. He turned himself the other way. The trembling and twitching stopped. He supposed he could descend tail-first, but that struck him as ignominious. Might there be tasty seeds in some of those pine cones *up* the tree?

He started to climb—and found he was a natural at it. But the higher he went, the skinnier the pine got. And the bark grew smoother, harder to grip. Then, to make matters worse, the tree began swaying—more than those around it.

Phoenix looked up and saw why. Their pine poked above the others, exposing it more to the wind. But this wasn't necessarily all bad. The topmost pine cones looked within easy reach, and there was something appealing in the idea of being above everyone else. But on his final push he made the rookie mistake of looking down.

A few weeks ago, as a newborn, he'd clung to his nursing mother, but that was nothing compared to how he clung to the skinny tree now. The needle-strewn ground was so far away! However, the wind gradually died down, and as the tree grew more stable, his panic turned to disgust. What kind of tree squirrel was afraid of heights? He lifted his eyes and edged upward.

Once perched on the highest branch, he was so pleased with himself that he even forgot he was hungry. What a view! Beyond the woods to the west was a town with buildings and steeples even higher than his pine. To the south, ponds and wetlands glimmered in the morning sun. Rising out of a newly planted cornfield to the north were giant towers carrying power lines on their steel shoulders. To the east, toward the sun, a bridge crossed a boat-speckled bay to a spit of land crowded with beach houses. Beyond that, an endless, silvery sea.

"Phoenix!"

Phoenix looked down again, but this time only three branches down. There was his father, Rupert, looking very stern—or trying to, anyway. Phoenix had assumed his family was asleep when he'd slipped out of the nest, but in fact his father had seen him. However, Rupert had done nothing to stop him. For much of March and all of April he'd dragged food home for the kits. Now that it was May he figured it was high time they got out and foraged for themselves. But then his mate had woken up, noticed a head missing, and had a fit.

"Get down here!" Rupert said.

Phoenix gulped and started a pathetic, tail-first descent. When he followed his father back into the nest, his mother gasped with relief.

"I thought you might have fallen out and broken your skull!" she cried.

"Hardly," Rupert said. "He went all the way to the top."

"*What!* Phoenix, you're only ten weeks old!"

"We're very disappointed in you," said Rupert. "You could have been picked off up there. Remember what we told you about birds of prey?"

Phoenix's brothers sniffed reprovingly, but Phoenix didn't mind. Though his father said he was disappointed in him, the gleam in his eyes said otherwise.

As the weeks went by, it became clear that Phoenix was the pick of the litter. He was the biggest of the bunch, with the most lustrous fur—a luminous

golden-brown on his back, pure white on his belly—
and by far the bushiest tail. He was the most venture-
some, too, and was first to move out and find a hole
of his own. It was only a few trees away. Squirrels generally spend their lives within a mile or two of where
they're born. So he still saw a good deal of his family,
often going to forage with his father. The central part
of their woods was mostly pines, but the outer fringes
had lots of oaks and walnuts and hickories. Rupert got
a kick out of showing him which nuts and acorns were
best and how to cache them cleverly so birds and chipmunks wouldn't find them.

Phoenix also became quite popular with his sisters'
girlfriends. He considered most of them empty-headed,
but one named Giselle made an impression on him.
She had an adorable white blaze on her snout and
was always carrying on about a young squirrel named
Tyrone, whom Phoenix took an instinctive dislike to.
Tyrone was reputed to live in a stump in the north end
of the woods, and one day when Phoenix was poking
around for food in that vicinity, they crossed paths. To
his dismay, Tyrone's fur was every bit as shiny as his. His
tail might have been even bushier.

"Huh," Tyrone said after they introduced themselves. "I always thought Phoenix was a girl's name."

Phoenix's fur prickled. "You live in a *stump*?" he said.

"Only when I'm slumming in the woods," Tyrone said.

Phoenix wasn't sure what this meant, but the next time he ran into his sisters' crew, Giselle explained that Tyrone had a second home.

"The attic of a house in town," she said. "Guess what he does there!"

"What?" Phoenix said unenthusiastically.

"Shinnies down a rain gutter at night and raids the humans' pantry! You wouldn't believe the cool stuff he brings back. Ever had golden raisins? Or smoked almonds? Last time he brought back red licorice!"

Phoenix had never had golden raisins, smoked almonds, or red licorice. In fact, he'd never seen a human. When he mentioned this to his father, Rupert assured him he hadn't missed anything.

"Tyrone raids their pantry," Phoenix complained.

"Is Tyrone a rat?"

"He's a squirrel, my age. What's a rat?"

"You don't want to know."

Phoenix did want to know. It bruised his self-esteem to have such gaping holes in his knowledge. He kept pestering his father until one day Rupert, who loved a good laugh, stopped by Phoenix's tree and called up, "How about a little sightseeing, son?"

If no one was around, Phoenix climbed down his tree rump-first, but with his father watching he used a technique he'd been perfecting of going round and round the trunk at a slight downward angle. When he reached the pine straw, he explained that he'd been checking the bark for caterpillars.

Rupert, amused, led him out the west end of the woods into a dry meadow. This provided more amusement. It was a minefield of whirring grasshoppers that kept making Phoenix jump.

Beyond the meadow was a road. "Hilliard Boulevard," Rupert told him.

As Phoenix reached out to test Hilliard Boulevard's ominously black surface with a paw, Rupert yanked him backward. There was a terrifying roar as something enormous whooshed by in a blur.

"See it?" Rupert asked.

"What?"

"The human."

"That was a human?"

Phoenix couldn't believe how huge the humans were, and how fast. But Rupert explained that the human was *inside* the contraption. When another similar contraption roared by, Phoenix again missed seeing the human inside.

"What are they doing in those things?" he asked.

"Trying to squash us," Rupert explained.

"What do you mean?"

After scanning the sky for birds of prey, Rupert led him along the side of the road till they came to a grayish stain on the pavement. Only when Phoenix made out the ringed tail attached to it did he realize it was the remains of a raccoon.

"Do the humans do that to squirrels, too?" he asked, appalled.

"Ask your great-aunt Flo," Rupert said with a sigh. "Sweet as the day is long, Uncle Frank was."

Phoenix's great-aunt Flo was a legendary figure in the woods, so wise that squirrels made pilgrimages up her white birch to ask her advice. But this was the first Phoenix had heard about her flattened mate. Gruesome as it was to think of, it only intensified his desire to see what these human assassins looked like.

Rupert climbed a fencepost, looked both ways, and hopped back down. After scanning the sky, he gave a nod, and the two of them dashed across Hilliard Boulevard. On the other side they made their way along the shoulder, weaving through thistles and milkweed and trash. Soon another road crossed the first—another Hilliard Boulevard, Phoenix assumed. They turned right and pattered along underneath a hedge as sparrows and wrens twittered overhead.

The hedge ended at a third Hilliard Boulevard. This one was square-shaped and full of the monstrous killing machines, though here they were parked diagonally and were mercifully standing still. Giving them a wide berth, Phoenix and his father started across a stretch of grass where every blade had been chewed down to exactly the same length. There wasn't a deer in sight, but there must have been scads around.

The two squirrels stopped at a chain-link fence that separated them from the most horrifying creatures Phoenix had ever seen. Some were splashing around in a square pond. Others were lolling on the grass.

"Humans?" he asked in a hushed voice.

"Their watering hole," Rupert said.

The humans were not easy on the eye. They had no tails at all, and some dreadful disease had eaten away most of their fur. Rupert explained that their furlessness accounted for the gaudy rags they wore around their midsections.

"You'd think they'd cover up those bellies, too," Phoenix murmured.

"They're great eaters," Rupert said, pointing at a crowded concession stand.

Phoenix's nose quivered.

"Hungry?" Rupert asked.

Phoenix was always hungry. They circled around behind the stand, where Rupert pointed out a line of large containers where the humans dumped food they didn't eat.

"May we have some?" Phoenix asked.

"Help yourself. But you might want to look before you leap."

Rupert tried not to smile as he watched his son hop from a bushel basket onto the rim of one of the containers. Phoenix pulled out something odorless and held it up.

"Newspaper," Rupert said. "Inedible."

Phoenix jumped to the next container. This one was half full of savory-smelling things. But as he was about to drop down for a feast, he spotted a grayish worm wiggling among the goodies. When a creature came slithering out of the mound of food, Phoenix nearly tumbled backward. The worm was its *tail*! The creature wasn't oversize or repulsively furless like the humans, but there was something nasty about its cropped gray coat and beady eyes and pointed snout. Worst of all was the naked worm-tail. Phoenix turned and dropped back down to the ground.

"Lost your appetite?" Rupert said, succumbing to his smile.

"There's this disgusting thing in there!"

"You *said* you wanted to see a rat."

They headed home, Rupert nicely entertained, Phoenix's horizons sufficiently broadened for one day. When they got to the final Hilliard Boulevard, there was no fencepost to climb, so Rupert crept to the edge of the hard, black surface and pressed his ear against it.

"All clear," he pronounced, and they dashed across.

That evening, as Phoenix was settling into his nest, he heard tittering and poked his head out of his hole. Down below, one of his brothers was walking with one of his sisters.

"Where were you?" Phoenix asked.

"Watching Tyrone," his sister said, looking up dreamily.

"What an aerialist!" his brother gushed.

"What a squirrel," his sister said with a sigh.

This left a sour taste in Phoenix's mouth, but it also piqued his curiosity, and late the next afternoon, while he was nibbling some purple berries, he spotted Giselle's silvery tail in a posse of young squirrels heading north. He shadowed them. They stopped at the edge of the woods and stood around chattering. When the sun began to set, they ventured out under the open sky, climbing a split-rail fence and sitting in a row on the top rail. Phoenix snuck over and climbed onto the lower rail. Beyond a dirt road was the cornfield he'd seen from the top of his parents' pine.

Suddenly Giselle cried, "Look, there he is!"

Phoenix figured the game was up. But she wasn't looking down at him. Nobody was. They all seemed to be focused on the steel pylons rising above the cornfield. Squinting, Phoenix made out a figure on one of the power lines stretched between two of the towers.

It was definitely Tyrone, his bushy tail silhouetted against the darkening sky. The mere thought of tightrope-walking at such a height curdled Phoenix's stomach. And Tyrone did more than tightrope *walk*. He burst into a sprint, racing the whole length of a cable from one pylon to the next. The squirrels on the top rail shrieked with delight. A catbird perched on one of the fence posts whistled in admiration.

"Is he the most stupendous squirrel ever, or what?" cried Giselle.

As the squirrels joined in a chorus of agreement, Phoenix felt as if he was going to be sick. Really sick. Were the purple berries poisonous? When a retching sound escaped him, the squirrels on the top rail all peered down.

"Hey, it's Phoenix," said one of his sisters.

"What are you doing here?" asked one of his brothers.

"By the look of it," said Giselle, "he's puking."

2

RED LICORICE

EVEN AS A NEWBORN PHOENIX HAD NEVER THROWN up. His mother had remarked on it. But now a purplish goo spewed out of his mouth.

He dropped to the ground and fled into the woods. He managed to snag an oak leaf without breaking stride, but as he was wiping his snout, he smacked into a rock and landed sprawled on the ground. Lifting his head, he heard chortling. Two chipmunks were enjoying the spectacle from a nearby log. The pair cheered extravagantly as he dragged himself to his feet. Humiliation complete, Phoenix staggered on to his tree, climbed to his hole, and curled up in his nest like a kit.

Of course, he couldn't sleep. His only hope, in fact, was that he was asleep already and having a terrible dream. He thumped the side of his head with a paw. This didn't wake him up. Neither did poking himself with a pine needle. The nightmare was real. He'd blown his berries in front of Giselle and everyone else.

After a while he heard claws on the bark of his tree.

"Phoenix?" came a concerned voice. "Are you all right?"

His youngest sister peered into his hole. She was the runt of the litter and the sweetest of the bunch.

"Just ate some bad berries," he muttered.

"Can I get you anything?"

"Thanks, but no." Then he swallowed his pride and asked if Giselle had commented on his "performance."

"Not yours," she said. "Just Tyrone's."

This did not lift his spirits.

In the course of the first sleepless night of his life, Phoenix came to a bitter conclusion. He could never show his face again unless he climbed one of those towers and did a high-wire act of his own. He knew why Tyrone chose the end of the day. Birds of prey couldn't see as well at sunset—except maybe owls—and the semi-darkness added to the drama. So he would have to do it at sunset.

He stayed holed up that day. His youngest sister dropped by midafternoon with an acorn, but the thought of the skinny cable so high above the ground had wrecked his appetite. When he finally ventured out, at twilight, a lot of squirrels were heading north, which made him think Tyrone might be at it again. But instead of trailing them he made his way to a half-rotted log that collected rainwater, and scrubbed his snout in case it was still vomit-stained. After that he dawdled some more. By the time he got to the northern edge of the woods, the sun had sunk behind a cloud bank. He crept out under the fence where the squirrels and the catbird were perched. The only creatures he could see on the power lines were a couple of redwing blackbirds. But when he checked the two nearest pylons, he spotted a squirrel making his way up one of them.

"Why does he have a rope over his shoulder?" came a voice from above.

"It's red licorice," Giselle said knowledgably. "Probably for quick energy."

Taking a deep breath, Phoenix got a bead on the

other tower and shot across the dirt road into the cornfield. The corn was thick and high, so it was quite dark at the base of the stalks, but today he kept his wits about him. He hurdled a garter snake and spooked a family of buntings, but managed not to run into anything.

When he reached one of the legs of the tower, however, he found he couldn't sink his claws into the steel. Assessing the situation, he saw that the crisscrossing braces formed a sort of ladder, and he started clambering upward, rung by rung. By the time he reached the spot where the tower's legs came together, two thirds of the way up, his heart was beating so fast he had to stop. He knew better than to look down. But when he looked up, there was Tyrone, out on one of the cables—using the red licorice as a jump rope! At first Phoenix was agog in spite of himself. Then he had an evil inspiration.

Two crossbars crowned the tower, each supporting two cables. Tyrone was on one of the higher cables. When Phoenix made it to the lower crossbar, the way up was blocked by a large metal box. But it was mounted on one side of the pylon, so by shifting to the other side he was able to climb the last harrowing stretch. The top of the metal box, level with the top crossbar, gave him a safe place to squat and catch his breath as he took in the spectacular view. Beyond the lit-up beach houses on the spit to the east, a silver trail led to a full moon rising over the ocean, while in the other direction the town glowed under a brilliant, berry-stained sky. But his focus soon narrowed to Tyrone's cable. If he could just give it a good jiggle, the miserable show-off might lose his balance and fall. But would he dare do it?

As Phoenix was working up his nerve to crawl out to the end of crossbar, the wind stiffened. He had to grab the side of the box to keep from blowing off. And it wasn't just a gust. The wind grew stronger and stronger, blowing the fur flat against his back.

He heard a shriek. Tyrone wasn't jumping rope anymore—he was dangling from the cable by his fore-paws! The wind was blowing him almost sideways. With another shriek Tyrone lost his grip.

Phoenix had wanted Tyrone to fall off, but the reality of it left him horrorstruck. Then he heard a third shriek. Peering over the edge of the box, he saw that Tyrone hadn't fallen all the way to the ground. He'd managed to catch one of the lower cables. He was hanging off it upside down, clinging with all four paws. Forgetting the wind, Phoenix hustled bottom-first down to the lower crossbar and squirmed out to the cable.

"Here!" he cried.

Tyrone looked around in surprise and started clawing his way up the sagging cable. But as he neared the crossbar, his back paws lost their grip, leaving him dangling by only his forepaws.

"Grab my tail!" Phoenix yelled.

Clutching the crossbar, Phoenix set his back paws on the precarious cable and lowered his tail. But he wasn't prepared for Tyrone actually grabbing it. The extra weight nearly broke his grip—nearly, but not quite. With a supreme effort Phoenix pulled himself fully onto the crossbar, and Tyrone scrambled up beside him.

"We've got to . . . get out of this . . . this gale!"

Tyrone panted, and he hopped toward the metal box.

An insulated cable ran into the box through an opening on the side. There was just enough room for a squirrel to squeeze through, and Phoenix wriggled in behind Tyrone. As Phoenix's eyes adjusted to the interior darkness, he made out various wires and switches and circuits.

Tyrone, perched on one of the switches, was gaping at him. "What the heck are you doing up here?"

Phoenix settled on a coil of wire. "I was curious to see what it was like," he said, not entirely untruthfully.

"Well, you saved my life, squirrel!"

He had, hadn't he? He found himself disliking Tyrone a little less. The box made a fine shelter from the storm, and the two of them huddled there till the wind stopped whistling in the opening. When they squeezed out, it was full-fledged night. Tyrone headed straight down the tower. Phoenix used his round-and-round technique. When he reached the bottom, he was chagrined to find the whole gang there to greet him. But before anyone could make a crack about his odd method of descent, Tyrone slapped him on the back and said, "This guy saved my fur!"

"We saw!" Giselle cried.

"That's my brother," Phoenix's oldest sister confided to a friend.

On the way back through the cornfield, squirrels vied to walk next to Phoenix. He barely felt the ground under his paws. Yesterday's humiliation was totally forgotten. He'd become a hero without even having to go tightrope-walking!

Back in the woods Tyrone ducked into the hole in his stump. He darted back out and dropped four nuts into Phoenix's paw.

"Small token of my thanks," he said.

The delicious smell made Phoenix's nose twitch. "What are they?" he asked.

"Smoked almonds. If you ever want more, just ask."

Tyrone thanked him again, said goodnight, and retired back into his stump. The rest of them drifted into the pines, Giselle falling in at Phoenix's side. He figured she wanted one of the smoked almonds, but when he offered her one, she said she never ate right before bed.

"Though I'm so wound up," she added, "I doubt I'll sleep."

He was wound up too. When she asked if he'd be interested in seeing her favorite spot, he said he'd love to.

"Meet me in a few at the burial ground," she said, and scampered off.

Seeing as he wasn't going to bed yet, he figured it would be okay to sample an almond. It was so tasty that he ate two more on the way back to his tree. He stashed the last one in his nest before heading for the burial ground.

This was at the very south end of the woods, just above the wetlands, where the soil was softest. It seemed a strange favorite spot, but Giselle was waiting for him by one of the stone markers, her fur neatly brushed. Before he could ask if one of her ancestors lay under the marker, she was scurrying out of the woods. He'd never been in the wetlands before, but he didn't hesitate, bounding beside her through the reeds. At first the reeds made a dry, rustling sound. Then they turned greener and quieter.

When he and Giselle emerged on the bank of a small pond, he realized *this* must be her favorite spot. It was beautiful.

"Look, another moon," he said, pointing at the water.

The moon was high in the sky now, and its twin glowed deep in the pond. There were stars down there too.

"Those are reflections, silly," Giselle said. She leaned out over the water. "See, there's me."

He leaned out as well. There she was! And him, too! He smiled at himself. He shifted around so his tail was over the water. It looked quite impressive.

"You have a wonderful tail," she said, as if on cue. "In the sunlight you can see a little auburn in it."

"Thanks," he said modestly.

In the past Tyrone had been all Giselle talked about, but as they crouched there by the pond, she kept bringing the conversation around to him, Phoenix. It was delightful. So was exchanging soulful looks. Just as he was wondering if she might want to brush whiskers, she settled the issue by doing just that. It was so nice that later, when they were saying goodnight back in the woods, they did it again.

Phoenix didn't get up the next day till the sun was high in the sky. It was the latest he'd ever slept, and he was so ravenous that he spent the whole afternoon foraging and eating. On the way back to his pine he thought of making a detour to the pond—it would be nice to check out his reflection in the daylight—but as he veered south he ran into a cousin of his who surprised him with the news that Tyrone was going tightrope-walking again.

"Why?" Phoenix asked.

"His licorice."

Phoenix followed his cousin to the north end of the woods. Most of the young squirrels were there already, Tyrone and Giselle included, Tyrone staring grimly out at the cornfield. High above it his rope of red licorice was draped over one of the power cables. It must have caught there when he got blown off. To Tyrone it seemed like a badge of shame.

As soon as the sun began to set, Tyrone marched determinedly into the cornfield. Phoenix followed the others out to the fence and perched by Giselle on the top rail. When they spotted a bushy tail on one of the towers, Phoenix commented that it took guts for Tyrone to go back up there.

"Let's just hope you don't have to rescue him again," Giselle said, bumping shoulders.

The licorice was dangling from the same top cable Tyrone had started out on yesterday, and Phoenix couldn't help admiring the way he scampered right out onto the power line without a moment's hesitation. On the other hand, the way he wrapped the licorice around his waist three times and tied it off with a flourish seemed a touch flamboyant. So Phoenix wasn't sorry when Tyrone had to stop to catch his balance on his way back to the tower.

"Oops," said one of the squirrels when Tyrone had to catch his balance a second time.

"I hope it's not getting windy up there again," said Phoenix's youngest sister.

The wind generally died down at sunset, but for the second day in a row the sunset seemed to be fueling it.

The cornfield began to ripple. The power lines swayed. Tyrone was grasping his with all fours now, struggling to reach the pylon. Phoenix had the horrible thought that he might be expected to go back up there to help him. But Tyrone made it to the top crossbeam on his own, then scrambled down the far side of the metal box and slipped inside to wait out the blow.

"What's in there, anyway?" Giselle asked.

"Human things," Phoenix said knowledgeably.

Off to the west the town's glow was brightening. To the east a mist-veiled moon was rising over the lit-up beach houses. But the picturesqueness didn't keep the young squirrels from growing bored.

"I'm over this peanut gallery," said one, dropping to the ground.

Others followed suit. Phoenix liked the idea of heading to the pond but figured Giselle would want to stick around to make sure Tyrone got down in one piece. When someone suggested he'd probably dozed off up there, however, Phoenix broached his idea.

"If you want," said Giselle. "But it's not as good when it's windy like this. If the water's not smooth, you can't see yourself very clearly."

Just as Phoenix was agreeing that it made sense to postpone, the town lights all went dark. So did the beach houses. The only light left came from the shrouded moon.

"Do the humans all go to bed at exactly the same time?" someone wondered.

No one knew. But the scraping of the corn stalks in the dark made their fur crawl, and the last of them soon abandoned the fence. Phoenix walked Giselle to her tree and brushed whiskers goodnight.

In the morning he woke up hungry, as usual, and dug the fourth smoked almond out of a nook. It was so yummy he decided to take Tyrone up on his offer of more. When he got to the stump, the catbird was perched on it.

"Is Tyrone home?" he asked.

The catbird shook her head.

"Out foraging?" Phoenix asked.

"He never goes foraging," said the catbird. "His larder's always full. Last week he gave me three golden raisins."

"Is he at his townhouse?"

"He never came down from that tower."

Phoenix looked out at the fence and the field beyond. The corn stalks weren't swaying anymore. "I guess he needed to catch up on his sleep," he said.

"You could put it that way," the catbird said.

"What do you mean?" Phoenix said, struck by the bird's dark tone.

"He's dead," said the bird.

"Dead?" Phoenix said incredulously. "What makes you say *that*?"

"I flew up and looked."

For a moment Phoenix just stared out at the nearest pylon. Had Tyrone been flattened like the raccoon his father showed him? What could have flattened him up there?

"I don't believe you," he said at last.

The bird ruffled its feathers. "Check for yourself."

3

SMOKED ALMONDS

PHOENIX'S PARENTS HAD DRUMMED INTO HIS HEAD never to leave the woods alone in the daylight, so he went to hunt down his father. He finally found him, paws on hips, frowning at a hole between two roots of a swamp maple.

"What's the matter?" Phoenix asked.

"Chipmunks," Rupert muttered. "That was one of my biggest caches."

Phoenix sympathized, then told him about Tyrone.

"Dead?" Rupert said dubiously.

Phoenix led him back to the vacant stump and pointed at the tower.

"Why would he be stupid enough to climb up there?" Rupert asked.

"You'd be surprised," said the catbird, alighting on the stump. "He's not the only one."

Phoenix stared daggers at the bird, who quickly fluttered off into a scrub oak. Turning to his father, Phoenix said, "Tyrone may be a showboat, but we've got to see if he's dead or alive."

Rupert scanned the sky carefully before giving the okay to make a dash for the cornfield. On the way up the tower Rupert stopped to do five more sky scans, which struck Phoenix as overkill. The biggest bird in sight was a blue jay.

When they reached the metal box, Phoenix acted as if he'd never seen it close up.

"Hey, look, there's a way in over here," he called out.

He let his father go first, then wriggled in after. When his eyes adjusted, it was a relief to see Tyrone looking fine, asleep in a corner with the licorice still around his waist. When Phoenix called his name, however, Tyrone didn't respond. Nor did he react to being shaken. Rupert examined him and declared forlornly that the catbird was right.

"But he's not flattened," Phoenix said.

"You don't have to be flattened to be dead, son."

"So—what killed him?" Phoenix asked in alarm.

Rupert had no clue. "Your great-aunt Flo might have an idea," he said. "Go get her. And be careful."

Phoenix suspected this was a fool's errand. Knowledgeable as she was, his great aunt was the oldest squirrel he knew, and he seriously doubted she would be able to climb the steel tower. But he went, and when he got to her white birch, he wondered if he might be mistaken. Her hole was near the very top, and she clearly got up and down from there.

Phoenix's nest, like most squirrels', was made of leaves and grass, but Great-Aunt Flo's was lined with the same sort of newspaper he'd seen in the container near the humans' watering hole. When he poked his head in, it was almost as if she'd been expecting him.

"Ah, Phoenix," she said, smoothing her whiskers back against her graying snout. "Let me guess. Love problems."

"Er, no," he said. "My father asked me to get you."

"Having marital issues, is he?"

"No, it's about Tyrone. He's a young squirrel who—"

"I know Tyrone. Is it getting too much for him,

splitting his time between the woods and the town?"

"It's not that. He's dead."

"Oh, dear. Car?"

"Car?"

"Run over?"

"He's not flattened, if that's what you mean."

"Fox?"

"I don't think so. My father was hoping you'd come take a look. But . . . it's kind of high up."

"Then I'd better have a nibble first."

The aged squirrel pulled a half-eaten horse chestnut out from under some newspaper. After gnawing a sliver off, she offered it to Phoenix, but before he could even try it, she was out of the hole. He tossed it aside reluctantly and followed her. She hurtled straight down the slender white trunk and watched in amusement as Phoenix made his way down after her.

"You must be dizzy from all that circling," she remarked when he reached her.

"Admiring the bark," he said quickly.

"Ah. Birches are lovely, aren't they?"

When they got to the north end of the woods, Phoenix pointed out the pylon with the metal box.

Great-Aunt Flo muttered something under her breath about silly young squirrels, then she checked the sky and dashed into the cornfield. He bolted after her, but by the time he got to the tower she was already halfway up. His father's voice must have guided her into the box, for when Phoenix arrived, panting, on the first crossbar, she was nowhere to be seen. He felt a little shamefaced as he squeezed inside.

His great aunt and his father were examining Tyrone.

"Any ideas?" Rupert was saying.

Great-Aunt Flo didn't reply. But in a moment her ears pricked up.

"Hear that?" she said.

"What?" Phoenix and his father asked in unison.

She poked her head out of the box and quickly pulled it back in.

"Humans."

Rupert stuck his head out, then gave Phoenix a turn. A truck was approaching on a rutted dirt road through the corn. It stopped at the foot of the tower, and two humans got out. They had tool belts around their waists and shiny metal hats on their heads.

"They're coming up!" Phoenix cried, pulling his head back in as the humans started climbing the tower.

"This explains it," said Great-Aunt Flo. "Tyrone was electrocuted."

"How?" Rupert asked.

"I saw the lights along the beach go dark last night. He must have shorted their grid." She pointed out how Tyrone's body lay between two metal coils. "The humans are coming to troubleshoot."

Phoenix had no idea what "shorted their grid" or "troubleshoot" meant, but he was too nervous about facing humans to ask. "Shouldn't we get out of here?" he said.

"And leave Tyrone to the humans?" chided Great-Aunt Flo. "Don't you think he deserves a proper burial?"

Rupert peeked out of the box again. "At least they're slow climbers," he said. "How do we get Tyrone down?"

"Drop him?" Phoenix suggested.

"No, we'll strap him to your back, Phoenix," Great-Aunt Flo said.

"*What?*"

"You're the biggest and strongest of us."

"I daresay you're right, Flo," said Rupert.

Phoenix was stunned. Was he really bigger and stronger than his father? Dire as the situation was, the thought made his chest swell.

Great-Aunt Flo pulled the licorice rope from around Tyrone's waist but decided it wasn't strong enough. She yanked some wire from the spool.

"You probably have the strongest teeth, too," she said, holding it out to Phoenix. "Give it a try."

Squirrels are great gnawers. Their front teeth never stop growing, so they have to do a lot of gnawing just to keep their teeth from getting too long. Though the wire was very hard, Phoenix managed to sever it. He and Rupert push-pulled Tyrone out onto the crossbar, then Rupert and Great-Aunt Flo used the wire to cinch Tyrone onto Phoenix's back.

Rupert was right about the humans being slow. In all this time they'd barely managed to get halfway up one of the tower's legs. They were unobservant as well. As they clanged upward, they didn't even notice the three squirrels—four, if you counted Tyrone—making their descent on the opposite side of the tower. Of course Phoenix went backward the whole way down.

"Out of respect for Tyrone," he explained to his father and great-aunt at the bottom.

Their descent hadn't gone unnoticed by the squirrels. Several had been struck earlier by the sight of the great and wise Flo racing north through the woods with young Phoenix on her heels. Now almost every squirrel in the area had gathered by Tyrone's stump as a welcoming party. The scene quickly turned lugubrious. Tyrone's relatives gnashed their teeth and moaned as they unloaded Phoenix's limp cargo.

At twilight the squirrel community held a ceremony at the burial ground. Somber as it was, Phoenix couldn't help noticing the admiring looks he was getting from other young squirrels. If his rescue of Tyrone hadn't erased the puking episode from everyone's minds, his carrying Tyrone's body down the tower certainly had. Still, it sobered him to think that a squirrel as young and healthy as Tyrone could suddenly be lying six inches underground—even if Tyrone's mother said in her sniffling tribute that her son was now "in a place where all nuts are shelled."

After the burial most of the squirrels slumped off to their holes or dreys. Phoenix was about to join Giselle when Great-Aunt Flo linked arms with him.

"Would you walk me home?" she said.

"Of course!"

Great-Aunt Flo wanted to make sure he wasn't too traumatized by his friend's death.

"It is pretty horrible," he admitted. "How do you get 'electrocuted' anyway?"

"It has to do with electricity," she told him.

"What's that?"

"A power source vital to humans. It provides them light and heat."

Having displayed his backward climbing to her already, he wasn't about to display his ignorance, so he nodded as if he understood.

On the way home from his great-aunt's birch, he ran into Giselle, who wondered if he felt like going to the pond. He did. After all the looks he'd been getting, it would be nice to check his reflection to see if he looked any different, plus it would be comforting to snuggle with Giselle. But somehow it didn't seem right in the wake of the funeral, so he suggested they hold off till tomorrow.

"Maybe you're right," she said with a sigh.

* * *

When he came down his pine the next morning, a portly uncle of Tyrone's was waiting for him on the pine straw.

"Quite the circler," the uncle commented.

"Morning exercise," Phoenix explained. "May I help you?"

"We've been dividing up the poor lad's things. Seeing as you brought him back to us, we thought you should have a memento."

He handed over a foil pouch. Phoenix opened it. Out wafted the delightful smell of smoked almonds.

"Thank you! I'll think of Tyrone every time I eat one."

He stowed the pouch in his hole but stuck a couple of the almonds in his cheek before going to look for Giselle. When he found her by the burial ground, he wondered if she might have been communing with Tyrone. But her mood seemed awfully bouncy for that.

"Last one to the pond's a chipmunk!" she cried.

Off they went, racing out of the woods into the reeds. She was almost as fast as Great-Aunt Flo, and though he sprinted full-out, she nipped him, bursting out of the reeds onto the bank of the pond a tick before he did.

"Did you let me win?" she asked, once she caught her breath.

He tried to smile enigmatically—not easy while panting. After a moment they heard a soft croak.

"A bullfrog," Giselle said, pointing across the pond. "Ever had frog?"

He shook his head.

"Me neither," she said. "I had salamander once."

"How was it?"

"Chewy. Isn't it a gorgeous day? Not a breath of wind."

Nuzzling against him, she gave him one of her soulful looks.

"Your breath's funny," she said after they brushed whiskers.

"Probably these," he said, spitting the smoked almonds into a paw. "One's for you."

"Out of your mouth?" she said, wrinkling her nose.

"Oh, sorry."

He went to the water's edge and washed the almonds. As he turned back, he caught a glimpse of his tail in the pond and couldn't resist swiveling back around and leaning out over the water. He gave his tail a fluffing shake. It was terrible that Tyrone was gone, but at least there could be no question now who was the finest specimen of young squirrelhood in the woods.

"You know," he said, "in the daytime you can see yourself even better in the—"

A searing pain shot through his left shoulder.

Phoenix felt himself jerked upward, the almonds falling out of his paw. He caught a glimpse of Giselle gaping up at him. In another instant she looked smaller than a chipmunk. Then she was no bigger than an acorn.

4

FRESH SQUIRREL

IN NO TIME THE WOODS WERE DIZZYINGLY FAR below, the pines like blades of grass. Phoenix twisted his head around and choked on a snoutful of feathers. He was in the clutches of a bird of prey. He tried to wrench himself free, but the bird tightened its grip, and the terrible pain in his shoulder redoubled—a talon was piercing it. The bird's other claw had a vicelike hold on his hindquarters.

"Let me go!" he cried.

The bird gave a great flap of its broad wings and said, "Are you a flying squirrel?"

"I'm a tree squirrel!"

"Then I don't think you'd want me to let you go."

Phoenix couldn't look down again. He couldn't look anywhere—they were too horrifyingly high—so he squeezed his eyes shut. With his eyes closed the sting in his shoulder seemed even more intense. Was he about to die? The air was rushing by faster than when he'd rescued Tyrone on the tower, and his heart was beating so fast it felt like it was going to burst out of him.

He went limp, waiting for the end. If the talon in his shoulder didn't kill him, the bird would soon land somewhere and eat him. That's what birds of prey did, his parents said. What part of him would be the first course, he wondered. If only it were over!

But the bird just kept flying along. None too smoothly, either. They would dip, then the bird would flap its wings again, and up they jerked. Eventually the bird muttered, "Ever consider a diet?"

It almost sounded as if the bird expected an apology. Phoenix just clenched his teeth. But the suspense became unbearable, so he unclenched them and said, "Why don't you stop and eat me?"

"Pardon me?" the bird said.

Phoenix repeated himself, shouting over the rush of air.

"You're not for me," the bird replied.

"Who am I for?"

"The eyases."

"What's that?"

"The chicks."

"Arghhh!" Phoenix cried, picturing little birds of prey pecking him to death. "Couldn't you just put me out of my misery?"

"I can see your point of view," the bird admitted. "But they like their food fresh."

"Where are they?" Phoenix asked in a strangled voice.

"In the nest. More's the pity."

They moved jerkily along, passing a flock of starlings heading south. Then the bird said, "You're too young to have kids, I suppose. A word of advice. Don't be soft. Boot them out when it's time they fledged."

Phoenix had no idea what "fledged" meant, but he felt a spark of hope. Why would someone offer child-rearing advice if he was about to feed you to his kids?

"My shoulder," he groaned.

"What?" said the bird. "Oh, sorry."

The bird relaxed its grip for a moment, extracting the knifelike talon from Phoenix's flesh before regrasping him. Phoenix's shoulder felt only slightly better, but the bird's consideration seemed another good sign.

"Is your nest nearby?" Phoenix asked.

"I wish. Silly of me to load myself down. But you were such easy pickings—how could I resist? And you know how kids are. You can't come home empty-taloned. I was down visiting Mother in Cape May. A long trip, but that's where I grew up. You?"

"Me?"

"You a Jersey squirrel?"

"I'm a *tree* squirrel," Phoenix said, managing a little indignation even in his current straits.

"I mean, you've always lived in New Jersey?"

Phoenix had never heard of New Jersey. He didn't like sounding ignorant, but under the circumstances it hardly seemed to matter, so he asked what New Jersey was.

"That," the bird said, pointing his hooked beak downward.

Phoenix took a peek—and almost fainted. Far below them two seagulls were riding the wind. Far below *them* was a beach.

"I picked you up in Manahawkin," the bird said.

"What's Manahawkin?"

"A place in New Jersey. Don't you squirrels know anything?"

Phoenix didn't say another word for a long time. He just kept his eyes shut and his teeth gritted. Even with the pain in his shoulder dulled, it was extremely unpleasant, dangling in the bird's talons. Little by little the air began to smell less fresh, though the flight got a bit smoother.

"Not my favorite part of Jersey," the bird finally commented. "But at least we're picking up a nice little tailwind."

Phoenix snuck another peek. Below them were

more Hilliard Boulevards packed with killing machines winding between big boxlike buildings with skinny towers poking out of them. He asked the bird what was coming out of the towers.

"The smokestacks?" the bird said. "Pollution, mostly. This is what they call an industrial area. Over there, that's a landfill."

"A landfill?"

"A dump," the bird said with a sniff. "Awful stench—though seagulls like it."

"What kind of bird are you?"

"A red-tailed hawk. Name's Walter. What's yours?"

Phoenix twisted his head around backwards. Walter did have reddish tail feathers.

"Phoenix," Phoenix said.

Walter didn't make any cracks about it being a girl's name, so Phoenix asked him what place in New Jersey he called home.

"The Palisades," the bird said. "Just north of the city. Glorious spot. You should see the sunrise over the river from our cliff."

"I'd like to," Phoenix said hopefully. "What city is it north of?"

"New York City. Good grief. You're not going to tell me you've never heard of New York City?"

Phoenix didn't tell him, though he hadn't.

"That's it, up ahead," Walter said. "Not a place you'd want to live. A regular hive of humanity. Though a cousin of mine likes it. Nests on a building by Central Park. He's a publicity hound. Got his picture in the newspapers."

Much of this was lost on Phoenix, but he did know what newspapers were and mentioned that his great-aunt lined her den with them.

"They don't hold up in the rain," Walter said. "We tried some in the nest. Should be there soon."

The prospect of landing would have been appealing, if not for the hungry little beaks that awaited him. Instead of starting their descent, however, they seemed to be rising higher.

"One plus about the city," Walter said, "is that the concrete holds in the heat, so when you do a flyover, you get some nice thermals."

"What are thermals?" Phoenix asked.

"Updrafts. Saves you energy. Quite a view, no?"

Almost against his will Phoenix took another peep. Below them was the most appalling sight he'd ever seen. From the top of his parents' pine he'd seen a dozen or so buildings and steeples, but now, directly below them, were millions—more spires than trees in the woods, all poking up at them like spears.

"This part of the city's called Manhattan," Walter said.

"Isn't that where you picked me up?"

"Not Manahawkin, *Manhattan*. It's an island. See the bridges? You can perch on them and fish in the river—if you're partial to fish. Personally, I'm not, but the eyases are."

Phoenix couldn't bear to look down again, even to see bridges. "Are the eyases partial to squirrel?"

"Um, well, yes. I'm afraid they are."

The hawk sounded almost regretful. So Phoenix couldn't help but ask, "You wouldn't really feed me to them, would you, Walter?"

Walter considered. In fact, he was rather enjoying his passenger's company, though it would have been nice if the squirrel were a trifle lighter.

Phoenix heard a noise and looked back. A bird a hundred times bigger and shinier than Walter was roaring toward them.

"Watch out!" Phoenix cried.

Walter swung his head around and let out a squawk. Flapping his wings in panic, the hawk loosened his grip for an instant, and Phoenix slipped from his claws. For a heart-stopping moment Phoenix was staring up at the gigantic shiny bird, which was blotting out the sun. The huge thing must have eaten Walter, for there was no sign of the hawk or his red tail.

Then Phoenix flipped over so he would land on his paws. But the ground wasn't there—only the spearlike spires rushing toward him. Off to his left was some of the water that surrounded Manhattan. He hadn't lied when he'd said he was no flying squirrel, but he instinctively mimicked one, spreading his arms and legs wide to create the most possible wind resistance. He strained to get to the water, which was bound to make a softer landing place than this city.

But he could tell he wasn't going to make it.

5

BROKEN CRACKERS

CENTRAL PARK, WHERE WALTER'S COUSIN DID HIS hunting, is over a square mile of woods, fields, and ponds, right in the middle of Manhattan. The city boasts plenty of smaller parks, too. Unfortunately, Phoenix didn't land in any of them.

But his luck wasn't all bad. Some of the city streets are lined with trees, and Phoenix happened to come down in an old sycamore with countless layers of broad leaves to cushion his fall. And when he finally dropped out of the tree and hit the street, the pavement wasn't as unforgiving as pavement usually is. This particular block was being repaved. A road crew had just laid down a new layer of hot tar, which was still soft and doughy.

Nevertheless, the impact was jarring, to say the least. The force of Phoenix's touchdown splayed his legs, so he basically belly flopped. Though it didn't quite knock him out, he would certainly have lain there in a daze if the tar hadn't been steaming hot. However, it was. It would have fried him like an egg in a matter of seconds. His whole front side was instantly scalded, so he instinctively flipped onto his back. This was just as bad. When he leaped to his feet, the tar scalded his footpads.

To make matters even worse, the fumes from the hot tar made his eyes burn and tear up, so he could barely see. He could still hear, though. Humans on the sidewalk were yelling things.

"Is that a squirrel?'

"More like a rat, if you ask me."

"He's about to be a pancake."

Of course, Phoenix could no more understand what they were saying than he could see the approaching steamroller. But as the gigantic thing bore down on him, he could hear it, and the sound was terrifying enough to send him bolting in the opposite direction. The pavement that way was just as blistering, so he darted left—and ran smack into a curbstone. Half stunned, he dragged himself off the steaming pavement onto a sidewalk, where he was greeted by a sound even more terrifying. A professional dog walker was coming down the sidewalk with six dogs on leashes, and the sight of Phoenix set all six of them barking at once. Phoenix sprinted away—and knocked into something else, something with a little give. He blinked furiously. His vision cleared just enough for him to make out a fence much like the one at the humans' watering hole.

As he squeezed between the chain links, he almost passed out from the pain. His whole body felt as if it were on fire. If only he could dive into the pond where Walter had grabbed him! That's what he needed: water to cool him off. And to drink. His throat was dry as dust. He blinked some more and trembled to see huge monsters looming up ahead, some with gigantic teeth, some taller than pine trees.

"What's with you?" said a warbly voice.

Phoenix cowered back from the blurry silhouette of a good-size bird. "Are you a red-tailed hawk?" he rasped.

"Do I look like a hawk?" said the bird. "I'm a pigeon, for goodness sake."

"Do you eat squirrels?"

"Why do you ask?"

"I'm a squirrel."

"You don't look like one. Where are you from?"

"A place called New Jersey."

The pigeon gave a low coo. "Don't tell me you swam the river!"

"River?" Phoenix cried. "Where is it? Could you show me, please?"

"Want to swim home, do you? The river's not far. This way."

Pigeons are worldly, big-city creatures who like to think they've seen everything. But this one, whose name was Martha, had never seen a charred creature like this swim the mighty Hudson River. It would be something to tell her grandchildren.

She waddled off across the construction site. That's where they were. The monsters were actually pile drivers, backhoes, and cranes. Figuring the pigeon was his only hope, Phoenix followed her around a deep hole and then underneath a big pipe lying across two sawhorses. But when they passed through a rip in a fence onto another sidewalk, a bloodcurdling sound stopped him cold. The river seemed to be full of killing machines whooshing by at fur-raising speeds.

"I meant a river of water," he croaked.

"What else?" said Martha. "It's over there."

"You mean we have to cross this Hilliard Boulevard to get to it?"

"Hilliard Boulevard? What are you talking about? This is the West Side Highway."

Martha rarely gave traffic much thought, since she could fly right over it. But this poor critter was wingless.

"We'll have to wait for the red," she said.

While they awaited this mystifying event, they exchanged names. Before long the killing machines all slowed to a halt, and Martha waddled across the highway. Only the thought of reaching water induced Phoenix to follow. Though he still couldn't see very well, he could hear humans laughing from inside their machines.

After crossing the wide highway they had to stop at another narrower one.

"This is where they jog and bike," Martha explained.

At the watering hole and in the cornfield Phoenix had gotten the impression that humans were slow, lazy creatures, but here their blurry shapes were hurtling by, some on foot, others on two-wheeled contraptions.

"Where are they all rushing?" he asked.

This was something Martha had never been able to figure out. But she didn't like sounding at a loss, especially to a bumpkin from New Jersey.

"They're looking for food," she said.

When there was a break in the stream of humans, Martha led him across the jogging path. On the far side Phoenix whiffed water.

"Jump in," Martha said when they reached the waterfront. "That's Jersey over there."

Squinting, Phoenix made out a square cove hemmed in by two long structures and, far off on the river's opposite shore, the hazy silhouette of more buildings. Directly below them, waves were sloshing against a stone wall. The stone wall looked slick, and the drop to the water was longer than from the hole in his tree to the ground. Desperate as he was for water, he simply couldn't face another free fall after what he'd just been through.

"Is there better access on one of those?" he asked, pointing at one of the long structures.

"Not really," said Martha.

She explained that this whole neighborhood used to

be derelict and almost deserted, including the piers. But in recent years luxury high-rises had been sprouting up all over the place—some of the spears Phoenix had seen from above. They were packed with humans, as were the piers.

"That one was turned into a golf range," she said, pointing. "There's a gym up there, and past that, a skating rink."

None of this meant much to Phoenix, but pain trumps curiosity. "There must be somewhere I can get down to the water," he said.

Martha pondered a moment. "Well, there is one ratty old pier that hasn't been gussied up," she said.

As she took flight, the tips of her wings clacked together. She landed a ways down the waterfront on a railing opposite a park bench where a white-haired human was sitting. This elderly woman was known for distributing broken crackers from a bag. A savvy pigeon was already lurking under the bench, waiting to pounce. Martha was tempted to stay, but when she saw poor, charred Phoenix dragging himself toward her, the prospect of watching him swim the Hudson won out.

"This way," she said, taking wing again.

Staggering after her, Phoenix wished he'd been electrocuted like Tyrone. He could tell he wasn't going to last much longer, and having to drag his burned and battered body along was agony. Better just to throw himself in the river, he decided. But as he was about to do so Martha called out, "Right over there."

She was pointing her beak at the next pier. Phoenix blinked some more, trying to bring it into focus. Pilings that looked like the pines in his woods supported a long, low, dilapidated building that jutted out over the river. The windows were dirty or broken, and there were holes in the sagging roof.

"Ten to one it'll get torn down or fixed up before long," Martha told him. "There's an old, half-submerged dock at the end. I'll meet you there."

This news gave Phoenix a second wind, and as Martha flew out toward the end of the pier, he headed for the pier building's entrance: a huge sliding door that proved easy to slip under. In the shadowy interior, wooden shipping crates were stacked up to the filmy windows on both long sides. A strange chittering emanated from them. In the central open space was a steel drum with a pile of books and newspapers and magazines beside it, but Phoenix never made it that far. There was something so creepy about the rustling and chittering that he turned tail and slipped back under the big door into the daylight.

He checked the far side of the pier. A rough wooden beam ran the length of it. There was quite a drop from the beam to the water, so he hugged the side of the structure as he made his way along. His scorched footpads picked up several splinters, but he finally made it to the end of the pier, where a narrow ramp led down to the dock.

"See?" said Martha, who was perched atop a nearby piling.

The dock really was half-submerged. As soon as he got down to it, Phoenix scrambled over to the sunken side, submerging himself. The icy water was the most intense relief of his life. After a few moments he took a sip. The water was a little salty, but drinkable. While he was quenching his thirst, a wave swept over him. After the initial shock he found that his eyes actually felt better for the washing.

"Ready to go?" Martha asked.

"Go where?" he said.

"New Jersey."

At this particular spot the Hudson was over a mile across, and from such a low vantage point—Phoenix's head was just above water—he couldn't even see to the other side. Squirrels can swim, but they're far too light to swim long distances.

"I'd drown before I got halfway," he said dismally.

"You mean you're not even going to try?"

"Sorry."

This was deeply disappointing to Martha, but as she flew away her mind quickly turned to broken crackers. Her departure was so abrupt that Phoenix didn't even have a chance to thank her for bringing him here. The water really did feel glorious. But it was very cold, and eventually he had to creep back onto the dry end of the dock. As soon as the sun warmed him up, his body began to throb again, so he waded back into the water to renumb himself.

As he repeated this procedure, the sun sank closer to New Jersey and turned redder and redder, as if it too had been scalded. With the day about to end, he couldn't help thinking back on how it began. Getting a packet of smoked almonds from Tyrone's uncle, then strolling to the pond with Giselle. If only he'd taken his parents' warnings to heart instead of making himself "easy pickings" for Walter! Then he would still be home watching this very sunset with Giselle rather than suffering torments of pain at the end of a pier on a human-infested island. Every moment he was feeling weaker. He usually had ten snacks a day, minimum—but today he'd had nothing, not even the smoked almonds he'd washed in the pond.

He wondered if there was anything to eat up in that creepy pier. But just as he was getting desperate enough to go look, he heard voices and dashed back to the sunken side of the dock. With only his eyes and ears above water, he watched two creatures descend the ramp. In the dimming daylight he wasn't quite sure what they were. But when they reached the dock a shudder ran through him. Those ugly worm-tails. They were just like the creature he'd seen rooting through garbage in that container near the humans' watering hole!

"So beautiful," said one of the rats.

"Another day dying," murmured the other.

The two rats crouched side by side watching the sunset, much as Phoenix had just imagined him and Giselle doing. His shuddering turned to shivering. What had he ever done to deserve this fate? Pierced by a talon, dropped from the sky, burnt to a crisp, and now freezing to death. If only the sunset would hurry up and end so the repulsive creatures would leave!

"What are those long, skinny clouds?" asked the first rat, who sounded female.

"They're from airplanes," said the other, who was very soft-spoken but sounded male. "They're called contrails."

"Oh, look at that big boat! Isn't it majestic?"

"I think it's called a ship."

Ship or boat, its wake created what looked like a tidal wave to Phoenix, and it was coming straight at him. He tried to cling to the rotting wood. But the wave swept him off his end of the dock. As it dragged him under the pier, he managed to grab one of the supports. But when he tried to climb it, he found it wasn't much like a pine tree after all. It had no bark and was so slick he slipped and splashed back into the water. Though the wake had passed, leaving the water calm, he could see that his only hope was the half-submerged dock, now some distance away. As he thrashed toward it, he could feel the last of his strength ebbing. He spat out some water and cried, "Help!" but the cry was feeble, and as water refilled his mouth, he realized his ordeal was finally over.

6

ROQUEFORT

THE TWO RATS WATCHING THE SUNSET FROM THE dock were actually brother and sister. Beckett was weak-eyed from poring over periodicals, but his hearing was as sharp as Lucy's, and they both heard the feeble cry and swiveled around.

Rats are good swimmers. Very good, in fact. They've even been known to swim through long sewer pipes and pop up in humans' toilets. Neither Lucy nor Beckett would have done anything so unsavory—they were wharf rats, not sewer rats—but Lucy often took dips off this dock on hot days.

Unfortunately, it was quite dark under the pier at this point, and not even Lucy's sharp eyes picked out Phoenix's head before it sank for the last time. But all day long Phoenix's luck had been a curious mixture of good and bad. It was bad luck to get snatched by a red-tailed hawk, but good luck that Walter was decent enough to withdraw the talon from his shoulder. It was bad luck to get dropped from the sky high over Manhattan, but good luck to land in a leafy sycamore. Bad luck that the new pavement beneath the tree was steaming hot, good luck that it was fairly soft. It was bad luck now to get swept off the half-submerged dock by the wake from a passing boat, or ship, but good luck that the wake bounced off the stone embankment and soon came swooshing back, returning him to the same dock.

Lucy and Beckett wasted no time in dragging the soggy body onto the higher end of the dock. Beckett pronounced Phoenix dead, but this didn't keep Lucy from putting her snout right on his to suck the water out of his lungs. It actually worked. Phoenix coughed up water and sputtered something unintelligible before passing out in pure exhaustion.

"Let's get him home," Lucy said.

"But is he a rat?" Beckett asked in his hoarse whisper. "His snout's not very pointy."

"Of course he's a rat. And he needs attention. Look at that shoulder."

"What he needs is a last will and testament. Though he doesn't look like he has much to leave anybody."

"Help me carry him to the crate, Beck."

"Are you crazy? Mort would have a fit."

Lucy couldn't argue with this. She loved their father, Mortimer, but since the death of their mother he'd taken to drink, which brought out his temper. The reason Beckett's voice was so weak was that Mortimer had throttled him for rustling pages when he'd been trying to sleep off a hangover. However, Lucy wasn't going to worry about their father with this poor half-drowned creature in such dire condition. She grabbed Phoenix's legs and started dragging him backward up the ramp.

Beckett sighed. He much preferred mental exertion to the physical kind, but he had a soft spot for his sister, so he finally picked up Phoenix's hind legs, and together they lugged him the rest of the way up the ramp and through a sizeable crack in the end of the pier.

The noises that had given Phoenix pause earlier were rats moving around inside the shipping crates, which they used as homes. The crates near the tops of stacks were the most sought after, but with their load Lucy and Beckett were glad, for once, that they lived in a bottom crate. Theirs was particularly small, and crammed with books and magazines Beckett had borrowed from the pile by the steel drum. But at least their father wasn't home.

At the far end of the crate were their beds: three scuffed loafers. Beckett was flabbergasted that Lucy wanted to let this filthy thing convalesce in hers. But it was pointless to try to stop his sister when she set her mind on something, so he gave her a paw getting the creature into it. Phoenix barely fit. He was still shivering, so they tucked some rags around him. Lucy opened their larder—a dented cookie tin—and pulled out a piece of ripe cheese. When she held it under their guest's snout, he didn't react. Undeterred, Lucy kept waving the cheese in front of him. In time, his unimpressive whiskers quivered.

As he came around, Phoenix's first thought was that he was in the heavenly place where all nuts are shelled. He remembered drowning, so he knew he was dead. But as a horrible stench filled his nostrils it hit him he must have ended up in the other place.

Opening his eyes confirmed this. His vision had improved, but it was only an added torture to see that he was stuffed into a leather restraint in a claustrophobic box with a pair of rats. One of them was holding the smelliest thing imaginable directly under his snout. He shut his eyes and tried not to breathe.

"I'm not sure he likes Roquefort," Lucy observed.

"Good," said Beckett, who was partial to it.

Lucy went back to the tin and exchanged the

Roquefort for a quarter slice of slightly moldy Swiss. When she held it under the patient's snout, he tried to press himself deeper into the shoe.

"Told you he's not a rat," Beckett said. "All rats like Swiss."

Lucy was inclined to agree, Swiss being her particular favorite. But all she said was, "His shoulder really doesn't look good."

"No worse than the rest of him."

"I think we should take him to Mrs. P."

Phoenix moaned. The mention of his shoulder made it throb—and made him wonder if he was actually still alive.

"Aren't I dead?" he asked, cracking an eye.

"As good as," Beckett said quietly.

"Are you warmer now?" Lucy asked.

Phoenix was still shivering, but he did feel warmer, if hopelessly weak. Just getting words out was a major effort. He sucked in a few shallow breaths and asked: "What is this horrible place?"

Lucy tail switched. "I know it's a little cluttered," she said defensively, "but it's our home."

"You live in Gracie Mansion, I suppose?" Beckett added.

"Sorry?" Phoenix said.

Beckett repeated himself, but Phoenix had no idea what Gracie Mansion was. If he'd had the energy, he would have told them he lived in a pine tree in a beautiful wood. When the female asked what kind of rat he was, however, he managed to squeak, "I'm not a rat!"

"Told you," Beckett said.

Phoenix drifted off again. Sometime later he was awakened by a different voice, harsher and a bit slurred: "What in the blue cheese is that?"

"We pulled him out of the river, Father," Lucy said.

"Why?"

"He was drowning."

Phoenix opened his eyes again. The father was another rat, of course, but even more repulsive than his kids. His close-cropped fur was stained and dirty, and half his naked tail was missing.

"Why'd you drag him here?" the father said. "It's not crowded enough? Yuck. He stinks, too."

"That's not his fault," Lucy said. "His fur must have gotten singed, then it got wet. That's never a good combination."

Ill as he felt, Phoenix was mortified to think he smelled bad to a bunch of *rats*.

"You're not exactly rose petals, Mort," murmured Beckett. "Sucking old beer cans again?"

"None of your lip," said the father. "Just get that thing out of here."

"I'm busy," Beckett said.

"With what?"

"Reading." Beckett was lounging on an open book.

"That's all meant for the drum, boyo," the father said.

The wharf rats collected books and magazines and newspapers to burn in the drum to take the chill off the pier in cold weather.

"I'll return everything by the first frost," Beckett said.

"What's the point of deciphering that human dreck?"

"What's the point of anything?"

"I'll show you the point of something," the father said, snatching up a chopstick. "Now make that thing disappear."

"We're taking him to Mrs. P.," Lucy said.

"That old pack rat's welcome to him," Mortimer grumbled.

"Come on, Beck, lend me a paw," Lucy said.

Beckett crawled grudgingly off his book. It looked like it would be easiest to leave Phoenix in the shoe, so Beckett picked up the toe, Lucy the heel. They hadn't even reached the doorway when Beckett dropped his end, complaining of a pulled muscle.

"Your beau can help you," Beckett said, limping back to his book. "That's one thing he'd be good for."

Lucy gave her brother an exasperated look. "Junior's not my beau," she said.

"Your crush then. Whatever you call him."

Lucy walked out of the crate with a sniff, soon returning with a young male rat who was considerably more strapping than Beckett. But at the sight of Phoenix he shrank back, squealing, "What's *that*?"

"Lucy's latest project," Beckett said. "Enjoy."

"Please, Junior, just help me get him to Mrs. P.'s," Lucy said, lifting the heel again.

Junior's name was really Augustus, but since it was also his father's name, his parents called him Augustus Junior, which others shortened simply to Junior. Junior made a face but told Lucy to get the toe and took the heavier end of the shoe himself.

"Good riddance," her father muttered as they left the crate.

Beckett considered following them, not relishing the prospect of being stuck alone with his father. But Mortimer quickly crawled into his shoe for a snooze, allowing Beckett to read in peace.

7

TASTELESS BROTH

LUCY WAS AS GLAD TO GET OUT OF THE CRATE AS her father was to see her go. Junior lived in a beautiful, tip-top crate with an important father and a house-proud mother. Only in an emergency like this would Lucy have exposed Junior to her crummy home.

It made her feel a little better that they were going to see Mrs. P., for being able to claim Pandora Pack-Rat—the oldest, wisest, and fattest rat on the pier—for a friend was a feather in Lucy's cap. Mrs. P. lived on the ground floor too—but in her case by choice. After outliving her spouse and both their children, she'd reached an age and a weight that made climbing disagreeable, so she'd moved down from her penthouse to her current residence. It was the largest on the pier, consisting of six crates: four on the bottom floor, arranged in a square, and two upstairs. You entered a parlor furnished with satin cushions. In a back corner a stick for stirring paint served as a ramp to the two second-floor crates, which were occupied by a sewer rat she'd adopted named Oscar. The other bottom front crate was her "gallery." Pack rats are great hoarders, and Mrs. P. had a lot of treasures, some collected in her spryer days, some inherited from a legendary great-uncle of hers. The crate behind the gallery was where she kept her cheeses, mostly cheddars. Among rats, being fat is a sign of health and prosperity, and having a whole crate just for cheeses was an unheard-of luxury. But since she could cure almost any ailment, no one begrudged Mrs. P. her cushy lifestyle—except maybe Mortimer. Whenever he asked her for headache pills, she would just smile and advise less pub crawling.

Lucy and Beckett liked to visit her even when they were feeling fine, and pick her brain about rat history. Mrs. P. wasn't as familiar with Junior, however, so Lucy had him wait outside with the patient while she went in alone. The impressively plump rat was ensconced on the most cheese-stained of her cushions, a chunk of cheddar in one paw.

"Hullo, dearie," she said, her broad, gray face lighting up.

"Hi, Mrs. P.," Lucy said. "I brought someone to see you, though I'm afraid he's not in very good shape."

Lucy ducked back out the door, and she and Junior lugged in Phoenix.

"Mercy!" Mrs. P. exclaimed. "He looks as if he's been in a torture chamber."

Woozy as he was, Phoenix liked the huge rat instantly. That was just how he felt.

"Is he even a rat?" Junior asked.

Mrs. P. leaned over the shoe to examine Phoenix more closely. The amulet she wore around her neck hit his nose, and cheddar crumbs fell from her whiskers.

"He's so badly burned, it's hard to tell," she said,

peering closer still. "But my guess would be squirrel."

"I've seen squirrels," Junior said doubtfully. "They're weird-looking, but nothing like *this*."

"Can you help him, Mrs. P.?" Lucy asked.

Mrs. P. wasn't hopeful but vowed to do her best. She waddled into the crate behind her parlor, which served as an infirmary and dispensary, and Lucy and Junior followed with the shoe. The infirmary was dimmer than the parlor, with an array of bottles and jars and canisters lined against the back wall. In one corner sat a kerosene stove; in another, an oven mitt. Lucy and Junior transferred Phoenix onto the oven mitt and moved the shoe out of the room. Mrs. P. examined Phoenix from head to tail, clucking her tongue as she poked and prodded him.

"What on earth happened to you?" she asked.

Phoenix would have liked to tell someone about his nightmarish adventures, but at this point he was barely conscious, and the best he could do was groan. All it took was Mrs. P. touching his wounded shoulder to make him pass out.

"Would you like me to sit with him?" Lucy asked, sticking her head back into the infirmary.

"I suspect he'll be out a long while, child," Mrs. P.

said. "Maybe forever." Seeing the horrified look on Lucy's face, Mrs. P. added, "Are you friends?"

"Well, no," Lucy said. "But . . . can't you save him?"

Mrs. P. couldn't make any promises, but she worked on Phoenix well into the night. He never came to. She was dozing on a spool of white bandaging tape at his bedside when Lucy stopped by the next morning.

"Good grief," Lucy said.

The squirrel looked even more grotesque this morning. He was coated with a glistening ointment, and there was one bandage on his shoulder, another on his tail. Except for the slight rising and falling of his chest he could have been dead.

"Ah, dearie, I'm glad you came," Mrs. P. said, rousing herself. "My eyes aren't what they were. I washed his feet, but I was hoping you could do the splinters. My tweezers seem to have disappeared, so you might have to use your teeth."

This was an unappealing idea. Rats worry about germs like everyone else. But Lucy knew that splinters can fester, and that it would be best to get at them while he was still unconscious, since the extractions were bound to be painful. So she set to work.

She was on the third splinter of four when Phoenix moaned. A terrible pain was pulling him out of his coma. He opened an eye—and saw a rat gnawing on him!

"Hold still," Mrs. P. said as he howled and jerked his hind paw away. "Lucy's almost finished."

Phoenix looked in horror from the massive figure at the head of the bed to the cannibal at the foot of it.

"She's on the last splinter," Mrs. P. explained.

As it dawned on him what was going on, Phoenix calmed down and let Lucy, the young female rat from yesterday, turn back to his hind paw. As Mrs. P. waddled over to the stove, Phoenix gritted his teeth and focused on a little silver thing—a harness bell from a Christmas decoration—that Lucy wore on a bit of shoelace around her neck. He yelped when she yanked out the splinter, but the pain soon subsided, and odd as it was to be thanking a rat, he felt he should thank this one. First she'd pulled him out of the river, and now she'd pulled out his splinters.

"I just hope you get better," she said. "What's your name anyway?"

As luck would have it, Junior and Beckett walked in just as Phoenix told her.

"Phoenix?" Junior said. "Isn't that a girl's name?"

"This is an infirmary," Mrs. P. said, glancing over her shoulder, "not a convention hall."

"I was looking for Lucy," Junior explained.

"Just curious if our flotsam survived the night," said Beckett.

While Phoenix was wondering what "flotsam" meant, Mrs. P. came back to the oven mitt and handed him a steaming cup.

"Drink," she said.

Phoenix had never drunk anything hot before. When he tried it, he yelped again.

"I burned my tongue!"

"Now it matches the rest of you," Beckett couldn't resist pointing out.

Mrs. P. blew on the broth to cool it and coaxed Phoenix to try again.

"What's in it?" Phoenix asked.

"This and that," Mrs. P. said.

The broth was pretty tasteless, but Phoenix was too hungry to reject it.

"Do you have any nuts?" he asked when the cup was drained.

"Nuts?" said Junior. "Are you nuts?" He laughed, realizing he'd made a sort of joke.

"Such a wit," Beckett murmured.

After forcing another cup of broth on Phoenix, Mrs. P. announced that he needed bed rest. The three young rats cleared out, and Mrs. P. tucked a handkerchief around her patient. Phoenix actually did feel drowsy again, but before he could doze off another young rat slipped into the infirmary, this one smaller than the others, with oily, black fur and yellow eyes.

"Ah, Oscar," Mrs. P. said. "Are you busy?"

"Not if you need something, ma'am," Oscar said with a little bow.

"I could use a carrot for his soup, if you could scrounge one up."

Oscar's eyes narrowed suspiciously. "He's not a relative, is he?"

"Lord, no."

"A carrot it is."

When Mrs. P. and Phoenix were alone again, she explained that she'd found Oscar in a dumpster, the only survivor in an abandoned litter of sewer rats. "My own kids were gone, so I adopted him," she said. "Oscar's been a blessing. A born scrounger, and very attentive. Even empties the privies now that it's hard for me to get out."

"What's a privy?" Phoenix asked.

Instead of answering, Mrs. P. peeled back the bandage on his shoulder. The wound had too much puss. While she went off to make a poultice, the hot soup knocked Phoenix out.

When he woke up, he was alone. He had no idea how long he'd been unconscious, but there was something soft and moist on his shoulder that looked like a gob of chewed up leaves or grass. Though he still ached all over, he was feeling slightly better, and for the first time since Walter grabbed him, he wondered if he might somehow be able to get home. Giselle would have told his parents what had happened, so they would assume he was dead. His poor mother!

He thought of the bridges Walter had mentioned. When Mrs. P. waddled in, he asked if there was a bridge that went to New Jersey.

"I think there's one, a ways north of here," she said.

She heated him up another cup of broth. This time he had the strength to blow on it himself. He asked what time of day it was, since it was impossible to know with so little light leaking in between the crate's slats.

"Evening," she said.

"Do rats all live in wooden boxes?" he asked.

"No, no," she said, settling on the spool. "Just wharf rats."

"Someone said you're a pack rat."

Mrs. P.'s belly quivered with amusement. "There used to be wharf rats who looked down their snouts at us pack rats. But that all changed when a great-uncle of mine helped save the piers."

Long ago, she told him, the piers in this part of the city had been alive with human commerce. But when the great shipping lines had fallen on hard times, the piers became empty and derelict, and rats colonized them.

"Our golden age," she said. "It lasted generations. Such character the old piers had! Then came a terrible calamity."

"What's that?"

"Gentrification. Now most of the piers have either been torn down or spiffed up so you wouldn't recognize them."

"I guess it's lucky you have this one," Phoenix said.

She congratulated him on his attitude, telling him that patients who look on the bright side of things are the ones most likely to recover. And over the next few days Phoenix did continue to get better, though all he ate was the tasteless broth. The dim room encouraged sleeping, and he slept more than when he was a kit, even if there were times when Mrs. P.'s snoring woke him in the middle of the night. He learned how to maneuver himself onto the privy she put by his bed. Oscar, who had the job of emptying it into a storm sewer, called it "the can," and it actually was one, formerly meant for condensed milk. Mrs. P. applied the glistening ointment and changed Phoenix's poultice daily. Even in the dimness he noticed that what should have been fine white fur on his belly was still black and patchy, but Mrs. P. would pull the handkerchief back up and tell him not to fret about it. Lucy dropped by often, sometimes with Junior in tow, sometimes with Beckett, sometimes by herself. She usually brought a chunk of cheese, which Phoenix would thank her for and hide under the blanket. When she came alone, she perched on the spool and asked him about himself. It was a relief to tell someone about his horrific experience, and rather nice to see how impressed she was by his description of flying up the coast of New Jersey in the claws of a hawk.

"We rats are not at all fond of heights," she said. "I wouldn't have been able to open my eyes."

Phoenix implied that squirrels weren't a bit afraid of heights, glossing over the fact that he'd kept his eyes shut for 99 percent of the flight. She was amazed by his landing, too, saying she could just picture the close call with a steamroller. Unlike many wharf rats, Lucy had crossed the West Side Highway numerous times—to hunt down her father after he stayed out all night—and she'd witnessed some of the repaving that was going on in the gentrifying neighborhood over there. She was also curious about where Phoenix came from, and talking about the woods made him so homesick he sometimes had to fight back tears. Noticing this, she would promise to help him get across the bridge to New Jersey once he'd recuperated. After she left, he would toss the cheese into the privy.

One night when Mrs. P. was rattling the crate walls with her snores, Phoenix got himself out of his bed and onto his feet. His footpads were tender, his hind legs pathetically weak, but he managed to wobble to the parlor doorway. After taking a breather he made it over to Mrs. P., who was asleep on her back on her favorite cushion. When he nudged her, she rolled over and quit snoring. He staggered back to the oven mitt.

The next time he woke up, he heard Mrs. P. talking with Lucy out in the parlor and decided to give them a surprise. He faltered over to the doorway, took a couple of deep breaths, and stepped through.

"Sakes alive!" cried Mrs. P.

"Phoenix!" cried Lucy.

Junior, who was there too, wrinkled his snout as Lucy helped Phoenix over to one of Mrs. P.'s cushions. Mrs. P. offered Phoenix a piece of the cheddar she'd been nibbling on, but he politely declined.

"It's so good to see you out of bed," said Lucy, sitting beside him.

Junior sniffed and drifted into the gallery. Like the parlor, the gallery got a fair amount of morning light through the chinks, and the sight of all the treasures there turned Junior's annoyance to awe. Sorted in separate jars were bottle caps, corks, coins, washers, screws, campaign buttons, rubber bands, paper clips, and popsicle sticks. There were combs with missing teeth, brushes with missing bristles, barrettes, hair bands, scrunchies, hair ties, and bobby pins. A drinking glass was stuffed with pencils, fountain pens, ballpoint pens, felt pens, and Sharpies. There were keys, candle stubs, pairs of reading glasses, old cell phones, compacts, a shoe horn, a pocket calculator, and a fishing reel. There was a thick glass lockbox with bronze fittings full of precious items—lost earrings, wedding rings, engagement rings, pinkie rings, watches, charms, brooches. What most enticed Junior, however, was one of the compacts. It was open, revealing a mirror, and as he inched closer, he could see his reflection. But even though his gray coat had a nice gloss, his heart sank. By this summer he was supposed to be full grown, and even standing ramrod-straight he could tell he still wasn't close to his father's height. His father was his idol. Not only was he the pier's sergeant at arms, he was the longest and most muscular rat in the whole community.

So Junior was feeling a little dissatisfied with himself when he drifted back into the parlor and heard Lucy tell Phoenix that he was looking much better than a few days ago.

"Give me a break," Junior scoffed. "He looks like roadkill."

Phoenix asked what that meant.

"Come here, I'll show you," Junior said.

Phoenix followed Junior back into the gallery, where Junior guided him in front of the compact mirror. Phoenix shrank back in disgust from a particularly hideous rat looking back at him: dark and scabby with a terrible overbite. As he turned away from the repulsive creature, the rat turned too, showing its naked tail. Phoenix looked over his shoulder. *His* tail was furless, naked. As it dawned on him that he was looking into something like Giselle's pond, something that gave back his reflection, he went hot all over, then icy cold, then collapsed on the floor.

8

DRAFT BEER

WHEN PHOENIX CAME TO, HE WAS BACK ON THE oven mitt in the infirmary. The handkerchief was pulled up to his chin, and Lucy and Mrs. P. were hovering over him. He thought he'd had a grisly nightmare until he peeled back the handkerchief and pulled his tail into view. It was utterly furless. The revolting, ratlike creature really was him.

"Don't feel bad, Phoenix," Lucy said. "It's so muggy this time of year, you're better off without much fur."

He groaned. His lustrous fur and bushy tail were mere memories! And his teeth! Since he'd been on an all-broth diet, with nothing to gnaw on, they'd grown to an absurd length. He wished he'd missed the sycamore and ended up splatted on the pavement like that raccoon on Hilliard Boulevard.

Lucy coaxed him to get up and come for a little walk, but he barely heard her. Mrs. P. brought him a cup of broth, but he didn't sit up to drink it.

"He just needs time," Mrs. P. said, leading Lucy out of the infirmary.

Junior was waiting in the parlor. As soon as he and Lucy left the crate, she turned to him and said, "That was very mean of you—making Phoenix look in the mirror."

In fact, Junior felt a little guilty about it. But no one likes having his bad behavior pointed out, so he insisted he'd done Phoenix a favor. "You want him living in a dream world?"

"But he's been through so much already. You just made it worse."

"Why do you care about him? He's not even a rat."

"He's a fellow creature."

"So's that," Junior said, pointing at a cockroach nibbling on a discarded cheese rind. But after a moment he softened and apologized. "It's going to be a real scorcher, Lulu," he said, squinting up at the pier's filmy, sun-glazed windows. "How about a swim?"

She never much liked "Lulu," but it truly was a scorcher, so she relented, and they spent much of the afternoon on the half-submerged dock along with most of the other young wharf rats.

When she got back to her crate, Beckett was poring over a book. "No sign of Father?" she said.

"Just blessed peace and quiet," Beckett said.

Their father hadn't made it home last night. Beckett was sure he was just sleeping it off somewhere, but Lucy went to look for him anyway. Once, when he'd staggered home alone after one of his binges, a cab on the West Side Highway had hit his tail, which was why half of it was missing.

Lucy slipped out under the pier's sliding door, darted across the jogging path, and waited for the traffic signal on the West Side Highway. She knew the neighborhood bars on the other side, as well as the alleys behind them where her father liked to drain the dregs from tossed-out beer and wine bottles. But this afternoon there was no sign of him in any of his usual haunts.

On the way back from the last bar, a newly paved street made her think of Phoenix, so when she got back to the pier, she stopped to check on him. Mrs. P. was in the infirmary, but Phoenix wasn't on the oven mitt. Lying there in his place was none other than Old Moberly, the pier's well-fed, white-whiskered mayor. Two other rats lay passed out beside him on makeshift pallets.

"Heatstroke, evidently," Mrs. P. said.

"Oh, dear," Lucy said. "But what's become of Phoenix?"

"I had to move the poor creature to the fromagerie."

This was what Mrs. P. called the crate behind the gallery where she stored her cheese. It was mostly taken up by wheels of cheddar, though there was also a wedge of manchego, a goat cheese Mrs. P. saved for special occasions. Lucy found Phoenix lying on a folded piece of cheesecloth. Even for a cheese lover the smell in there was a little overpowering.

"How are you feeling?" Lucy asked.

Phoenix stared at her as if he'd never seen her before.

"Can I get you something to eat or drink?" she

offered. "I know you're not crazy about cheese, but I could get you some soup."

Same reaction.

"You need sustenance or you'll waste away and die."

"Good," he muttered, closing his eyes.

She crouched there quite a while, but he didn't open his eyes again, and watching him sleep began to make her drowsy. What with all the swimming and searching in the hot sun, it had been a long day, and as soon as she got home, she crawled into her loafer and conked out.

She woke before dawn. Beckett was in the shoe on her left, but the one on her right was still empty. She got up and shook her brother, worried that their father had passed out somewhere with heatstroke.

"Heatstroke?" Beckett said groggily. "Rats don't get heatstroke."

"Mrs. P. is taking care of three cases as we speak. Come on, Beck. We have to find him."

Beckett rarely accompanied her to hunt down their father. The truth was, he and Mortimer hadn't gotten along too well even before the throttling incident.

Beckett's theory was that their father blamed him and Lucy for the death of their mother, a delicate creature who'd never really recovered from the strain of giving birth to them. Mortimer was particularly nasty when he drank. But since he'd been missing for two whole days, Beckett went along now.

Outside the pier, the city skyline was still lit up, glimmering against an ashen sky. The jogging path was deserted, the West Side Highway a cinch to cross. A sour-smelling human was passed out in front of the first bar they checked, but otherwise the sidewalks were pretty much devoid of them. In the alley behind the second bar a sewer rat was nosing around in some garbage. Lucy asked if he'd seen a wharf rat with half a tail, but he just gave her a dirty look and popped down a drainage grate. Sewer rats were a surly bunch.

The sun came up. The rounds were going slowly because Beckett had to stop every other block to decipher the writing on a building or billboard or awning. Most of the buildings had lots of windows—the new luxury high-rises were almost *entirely* window—so when they passed a building with no windows at all, Beckett naturally had to try to figure out what it was. While he was staring up at a flag hanging from a pole under the high cornice, Lucy noticed Oscar creeping out of a deli across the street with his sack. She admired Oscar's loyalty to Mrs. P., but he'd always seemed suspicious of her, so she didn't call out. He hugged the edge of the buildings as he slunk down the block. At the corner he snatched a candy bar from a newsstand, shoved it in his sack, and moved on.

At last Beckett was ready to move on too. But only a few blocks to the west, he had to stop again to check out some writing stenciled on a green plywood fence.

"'Post No Bills,'" he read out.

"And that?" Lucy said, pointing at some other writing.

"'No Trespassing.'"

But trespassing was exactly what they did, for an alley cat came tearing across the street and chased them under the fence into a construction site. Lucy spotted a pipe, about six feet long, lying on the dusty ground between a stack of cinder blocks and a cement mixer. She yelled, "Follow me!" and wriggled in. The pipe was barely three inches in diameter, making it such a tight squeeze that, crouching in the middle, she couldn't turn around or even look over her shoulder to see if Beckett had followed.

"Beck!" she squealed.

Her less agile brother dove and hit the pipe snout-on. For an instant he saw stars. The stars cleared up just as the alley cat pounced. A claw grazed Beckett's back, but he darted to the other end of the pipe and squirmed in before the cat could grab him.

This left him and his sister face-to-face in the dark pipe.

"Can he get in?" Lucy asked tremulously.

"I guess we'll find out."

The cat certainly tried. But his skull was a hair too wide to fit in either end of the pipe. All he could do was prowl around outside, hissing. As the sun got higher in the sky, the pipe grew hotter and hotter.

"I'm dying," Beckett announced.

"He can't wait forever," Lucy said.

"He can wait till we look like that squirrel."

"Could we face him down?"

"Face him down? Do you have any idea what cats do to you?"

"Um . . . not really?"

"They maim and cripple you but don't quite finish you off—so they can have fun torturing you."

Lucy admitted this sounded bad. But by early afternoon the pipe had become so hot they had to twist over onto their backs to give their paws a break from the scalding metal. Every time they thought the cat might have given up on them, another menacing hiss wafted down the pipe. But it was a Saturday—the reason the construction crew wasn't around—and at around 4:00 the weekend watchman came by to check the site. He had a German shepherd with him, and all it took was one deep-throated bark from the dog to send the cat skedaddling.

Luckily for Lucy and Beckett, mixing cement requires water, and they found a trough of it by the mixer when they finally backed out of the sweltering pipe.

"Home," Beckett said, once they'd rehydrated.

But despite the ordeal, Lucy dragged him along to check one last place, a corner pub a couple of blocks to the south. The neon sign in the window perked Beckett up. He'd heard their father mutter the name—CLANCY'S—in his sleep.

They followed a pot-bellied human in the door and hid behind an umbrella stand. The pub was already doing a brisk business. Humans were leaning on a long counter; others were sitting on stools or in booths. Tiny ones, smaller than rats, were waving sticks and running around inside a lit-up box suspended over the bar. Large or small, the humans made a terrible racket, but the place was wonderfully cool—heavenly after the broiling pipe.

Lucy and Beckett didn't see their father anywhere, but they crept along the baseboard till they were under a cage with a colorful bird in it at the near end of the bar. Lucy was about to ask the bird if he'd seen a rat with half a tail when the bird peered down and said: "He's spreading the word, I see."

"Excuse me?" said Lucy.

"About the A/C," said the bird.

Always interested in letters, Beckett asked what "A/C" meant. Lucy repeated the question loud enough for the bird to hear.

"Air-conditioning," the bird said. "Mortimer loves it."

"Where is Mortimer?" Lucy asked.

"Hangs out behind the bar." The bird shifted an eye to the lit-up box and squawked, "Strike three, you're out!"

Getting behind the bar was no problem, for there

was an open space under a fold-up section of the counter for bartenders to go in and out. At the moment, two bartenders were on duty, one in motorcycle boots, the other in sandals. As they rushed around, the boots stomped and the sandals flapped, and after the pipe ordeal this was more than Beckett could face. But Lucy dragged him along a low shelf that ran along the back, just above a damp rubber floor mat, and despite the din they soon heard a familiar voice singing off-key:

> *What a slender rat was Belle,*
> *What a tender rat as well,*
> *When I lost her, fiddle-di-dee,*
> *I lost the better part of me.*

Farther along the shelf Mortimer had made a nest for himself out of cocktail napkins among some dusty bottles of brandy and sherry that no one ever asked for. At the sight of his two children he quit crooning and frowned.

"What are you doing here?"

"What are *you* doing here, Father?" Lucy said. "We've been worried sick."

"Speak for yourself," Beckett murmured.

"I live here," said Mortimer. "Can't take all those

musty books of his." He cocked his head at Beckett. "And the crate has no A/C."

While Lucy was digesting this, Mortimer grabbed a paper cup, hopped off the shelf, and dashed right between the feet of the booted bartender. High up above, the bartender was filling four mugs with draft beer. He held the mug handles in one hand and left the spigot open as he filled them, so trickles of beer spilled down onto the rubber mat. Or would have, if Mortimer hadn't been there with his cup. When it was full, he carried it back to his hideaway with great care.

"Oh, Father," Lucy said. "I hope you're not on an all-liquid diet. It's unhealthy."

Her father pulled back one of the cocktail napkins, revealing a pile of Cheetos.

"They put these doo-dads out for the customers," he said. "Try one."

Lucy did. It was scrumptious. Not even Beckett could eat just one.

"How long are you staying here, Mort?" Beckett asked.

Mortimer slurped some beer and licked the froth off his whiskers. "At least till the heat lets up," he said.

"Who knows, maybe forever. I have a bad feeling about the pier."

"Why's that?" Beckett said.

"I came back early in the morning the other day and saw a couple of humans skulking around. Never a good sign."

Wouldn't you miss us? is what Lucy wanted to ask, but she settled for the less pathetic: "Wouldn't you be lonely, Father?"

"Lonely? Are you out of your gourd? Think this place is mobbed now? Wait till later."

"I mean . . . for someone you can talk to."

"No worries. That parrot's a first-rate conversationalist."

Lucy was hurt. Mortimer could be difficult and curmudgeonly, but he was still their father. Beckett, on the other hand, rather liked the idea of the crate without him.

"Let's go, Luce," he murmured.

"So long," said Mortimer, who preferred to drink alone.

Lucy wanted to ask if his song was about their mother, Arabella, who'd once worn the little bell that she wore now. But before she could find the words, the big humans at the bar let out a deafening cheer for something the little ones were doing inside the lit-up box. Beckett covered his ears and turned away, so Lucy gave her father a forlorn look and followed.

At the end of the low shelf she stopped and tugged Beckett's tail. "What's that say?" she asked, pointing at a row of cans.

Beckett squinted at them. "'Mixed nuts, salted,'" he read.

"Are 'mixed nuts, salted' nuts?"

"Stands to reason."

"That's what Phoenix wanted. Let's take him a can."

"It looks heavy. We could never get it all the way to the pier."

"We can roll it," Lucy said.

Once they tipped one of the cans onto its side, it was easy enough to roll. But rolling it all the way from the bar to the door unseen would have been impossible, if humans were observant creatures. Luckily for the rats, they're not, especially when guzzling beer and watching baseball. Lucy and Beckett made it to the umbrella stand unspotted, and when a raucous group of young men from the golf range barged into the bar with their golf bags, Lucy and Beckett scooted out with their can.

It was dusk now, but after the chilly pub it still felt like a blast furnace outside. Fortunately, they were just a block from the West Side Highway. On the way they had to duck behind a fire hydrant to avoid a nanny with a stroller, but there were no humans waiting on the corner to cross. When the light turned red, the furious flow of cars stopped, and Lucy and Beckett rolled the can onto the crosswalk. They barely got it across the three uptown lanes before the light turned green, so they had to cower on the median strip as cars whizzed by in both directions. Eventually, the light turned red again, and they started across the southbound lanes, unaware that an SUV and a yellow cab were waiting to make a left-hand turn into those lanes from the side street. As the SUV bore down on them, Beckett yelped and made a mad dash for the far curb. Lucy was too intent on the can to let it go. When the SUV's huge front left tire missed her by just over the length of her tail, she froze, petrified. From the curb her brother watched in horror as the taxi headed right for her.

9

GREEN PELLETS

IF IT HAD BEEN JUST LUCY, THE CAB DRIVER wouldn't have swerved. In fact, he would have *tried* to hit her. One less rat in the world was always a plus. But the driver didn't see Lucy, he saw a metallic flash from the bottom of the can. Just that Wednesday he'd gotten a puncture and spent the better part of an hour jacking up the car and putting on a spare instead of collecting fares. So he jerked the steering wheel to miss the piece of metal.

The cab's undercarriage whooshed right over Lucy's head, leaving her stunned. Beckett sprinted out onto the highway and tried to yank her back to the curb, but even then she refused to abandon the nuts. To desert his sister again was unthinkable, so Beckett moved beside her and started pushing. Shoulder to shoulder, they got the can to the other side just as the traffic signal turned green again.

They caught their breath on the edge of the jogging path, watching sweaty humans galumph by on their mysterious, food-seeking missions. When there was a break, they rolled the can across. To get it into the pier they went to the spot where the bottom of the door was warped up a bit.

Beckett figured his sister deserved credit for the nuts, so after helping her trundle them up to Mrs. P.'s door, he said he was beat and headed for their crate. Lucy pushed the can into Mrs. P.'s parlor. Mrs. P. wasn't there, so Lucy rolled it through the gallery into the fromagerie. Phoenix was still lying on the wadded cheesecloth, looking thin and wasted.

"Nuts," she said, righting the can.

He stared at her with glazed eyes.

"They're mixed," she said. "There must be some you like."

It registered on Phoenix that Lucy had come into

the reeking room with a can, but he was too intent on dying to say anything. Lucy gave him an appraising look, then, discouraged, went off to the infirmary, where Mrs. P. was still busy with her patients. There were four now.

"Sorry to bother you, Mrs. P., but I wondered if you'd given Phoenix any soup."

"Oh, child,"—Mrs. P. waved toward her patients— "I've been up to my ears."

"This heat wave is terrible," Lucy said, eyeing the quartet of comatose rats.

"I'm not sure it's heatstroke. It may be something more insidious."

There was some tepid soup on the kerosene stove. Lucy took Phoenix a cup, but he didn't seem interested, so she left it on the floor and went home. Beckett was reading a pamphlet in bed.

"What's 'insidious' mean?" she asked him.

"Nothing good. Why?"

"Mrs. P. says her patients may have something more insidious than heatstroke."

"Hmmp," he said thoughtfully. "How did Phoenix like the nuts?"

"He didn't even notice them," Lucy said with a sigh.

The sigh turned into a yawn, and she crawled into her loafer and slept till Junior stopped by late the next morning. It was another scorcher, so Junior wanted her to come for a swim. She had a nibble of rock-hard Parmesan and went along.

Beckett wandered over to Mrs. P.'s. He knew her parlor well, but he'd never ventured into her gallery before. The collections impressed him. So did the cheese in the fromagerie. Phoenix was lying tangled in the cheesecloth by the can of nuts, which he hadn't even opened. Beckett strode over to him and gave him a cross between a nudge and a kick with a hind foot.

"Do you know what Lucy went through to get you these?" Beckett said, pointing at the nuts.

Phoenix just blinked at him.

"She nearly got herself killed on the West Side Highway. Least you could do is eat a few."

Beckett worked the plastic lid off the can and pulled back the foil. The nuts smelled better than he'd expected, so he popped one into his mouth before pushing the can closer to Phoenix.

As Beckett passed back through the gallery, the glassful of pens caught his eye. He'd been hankering to try his paw at fashioning letters. He found Mrs. P. in the infirmary, screwing the top on a canister of capsules, and asked if he could borrow one of her writing implements.

"Of course, dearie," she said with a weary smile. "Help yourself."

She looked exhausted, but her patients looked far worse.

"Lucy said they might have something insidious?" Beckett said.

She set down the pill canister and picked up a thimble. "I found that on Moberly's whiskers," she said, tilting the thimble toward him.

By the light from the kerosene stove Beckett could make out a tiny green pellet inside. He gave it a sniff. "Smells . . . good," he said.

"That's what makes it insidious. It's poison." Mrs. P.

tapped the canister. "I gave them all this antidote, but the poison may have been in their systems too long. I sent Oscar out to see if he could locate the source."

This was calamitous news, but not quite calamitous enough to put the writing implement out of Beckett's mind. He chose a ballpoint pen with ACME BODY SHOP on the side. When he got home, he started copying letters in the margins of a magazine. He soon felt as if he'd been writing his whole life and couldn't wait to show Lucy his *W*s and *Q*s.

Lucy was with Junior and the gang on the half-submerged dock. Hopping in and out of the river didn't get rid of her worries—her father's desertion, Phoenix's refusal to eat, Mrs. P.'s overflowing infirmary—but it eased them. The highlight of the afternoon was a sensational flip Junior did off a piling. This was all the talk as the young rats headed back up the ramp late in the day.

But the flip was forgotten as soon as they stepped inside the pier. The place was in an uproar. Lucy and Junior joined a group gathered around his father, who was standing on a phonebook near the metal drum. Augustus Senior cut quite a figure with his impressive chest and a sword stuck in the scarlet sergeant-at-arms sash he wore around his middle.

"This cannot stand!" he was insisting. "It's a violation of our rights as rats! Something must be done! We cannot allow . . ."

"What's he talking about?" Lucy whispered.

Junior didn't dare interrupt his father, but a nearby aunt of his told them that the so-called cases of heatstroke were actually cases of poisoning. Gulping, Lucy looked around for Beckett. In times of trouble the community traditionally turned to the mayor for guidance, and since everyone knew Old Moberly was in Mrs. P.'s infirmary, there was another cluster of rats outside her crate. But Beckett wasn't in that group either. Worried he might have gotten into the poison, Lucy scurried off to check their crate.

To her relief, Beckett was home. He'd found a pen somewhere and was using it to scribble on the back of a magazine, totally oblivious to the hubbub outside.

"Haven't you heard, Beck?" she said. "Rats are being poisoned!"

"Mmm, best to steer clear of green pellets," he said, looking up distractedly. He grinned and tapped his writing with the nib of the pen. "Know what this says?"

"What?" Lucy said, mystified.

"'Buy one, get one free.' I copied it from inside."

"Beckett, there's a crisis going on."

She forced him to put down the pen and tugged him out of the crate. The crowd in front of Mrs. P.'s was making such a clamor that Mrs. P. soon appeared in her doorway. To get through it she had to turn sideways and suck in her belly. The crowd gasped in admiration at her size, but even so, Mrs. P. looked uncharacteristically grave.

"I've tried my best," she said, "but it hasn't been good enough. Three rats, lost. And our mayor hanging on by a thread."

Rats sucked in their breaths in dismay.

"Where's the poison?" someone asked.

Mrs. P. turned and called: "Oscar?"

No response. But after a second summons Oscar came out lugging a very full sack, which he deposited at her feet with a servile bow. Poor Oscar wasn't happy about facing this mob. Being a sewer rat by birth, he was smaller and lower to the ground than these wharf rats and knew they considered him inferior. He wasn't happy about doing Mrs. P.'s bidding all the time either, though he never complained. As a youngster he'd figured he owed her for rescuing him and giving him luxurious accommodations—two whole crates of his own. Even after he came to the conclusion that she'd just wanted slave labor, the prospect of inheriting her treasures had kept him obedient and obliging. He especially coveted the glittering valuables in her lockbox. But while Mrs. P. was far and away the oldest rat on the pier, she remained annoyingly healthy. And her growing fondness for Lucy and Beckett worried Oscar no end. Would she leave her treasures to *them*? But this latest chore had given him an idea.

Mrs. P. thanked him and opened his sack so the crowd could view the contents.

"Oscar found these sprinkled around the front of the wharf," she said. "If you come across any he missed, don't be fooled by the enticing smell. They're deadly."

"The green pellets?" Lucy whispered.

Beckett nodded. Someone near them called out, "Who put them in front of the pier?"

Before Mrs. P. could respond, a buzz ran through the crowd as Old Moberly himself staggered out of the crate. Sick as he was, the stout, white-whiskered rat retained an air of authority. A niece of his rushed forward to support him, and even Augustus brought his listeners over to join the throng. But when at last Old Moberly spoke, his usually grand voice was almost as soft as Beckett's.

"You shouldn't be out of bed," Mrs. P. said firmly.

"My megaphone," Old Moberly rasped.

Frowning, Mrs. P. asked Oscar to fetch it. Oscar climbed to Old Moberly's topmost crate and brought down the megaphone—a small Dixie cup with the bottom gnawed out. Old Moberly thanked him and, raising it to his snout, brought the assembly to order.

"May I ask," he said, "if any here present has sighted a human being in proximity to our pier?"

Lucy and Beckett exchanged a look. Their father's nocturnal habits were an embarrassment, but under the circumstances Lucy felt compelled to speak up.

"Um, our father says he saw some humans 'skulking around the pier' recently," she said. "Very early in the morning."

"Where would Mortimer be?" Old Moberly asked. "I would be interested to hear more."

"Um, he's not here at the moment, sir," Lucy said.

"Have there been any other viewings of humans?" Old Moberly asked, scanning the crowd.

"Oscar tells me he saw one outside the pier while he was collecting the poison," Mrs. P. said.

All eyes shifted to Oscar. Speaking in front of all these wharf rats was beyond him, but he managed to mutter something to Mrs. P.

"He says the human was sticking a notice up on the door," Mrs. P. relayed.

"Probably just one of their advertisements," said Augustus. "They put them everywhere."

"Go look," Lucy whispered to her brother.

As Beckett made his way through the crowd, Old Moberly told the rats it was "imperative to be extra vigilant henceforth." But even with the megaphone his voice was reedy, and as he was floating the idea of posting a round-the-clock watch for human intruders, he suddenly collapsed. The rats were aghast—except for Augustus, who experienced a little thrill. Though grateful to the mayor for appointing him sergeant at arms, Augustus was of the opinion that Old Moberly should have retired some time ago, paving the way for a special mayoral election in which he would be the clear favorite. He may have lacked Old Moberly's eloquence, but he was younger and healthier and certainly *looked* more like a leader of rats. Not that he wished harm on anyone. But if the old rat was too stubborn to step aside, ill health would have to do.

Following Mrs. P.'s instructions, Oscar helped Old Moberly's niece drag the mayor back to the infirmary. Mrs. P. followed. By the time she reappeared, Beckett was back, squeezing his way through the crowd to Lucy. When he told his sister what he'd seen, she cried out: "Beck deciphered the notice!"

"My hind foot," said Junior.

Other young rats scoffed too. But Mrs. P. motioned Beckett up to her.

BEWARE
RAT POISON
KEEP OUT
PiER DEMOLITION
COMMENCES AUGUST 28

"Pipe down!" Mrs. P. said as Beckett joined her.

The crowd quieted somewhat, but when Beckett spoke, few could hear. Mrs. P. shushed them again.

"The top of the notice is bubbles," Beckett said as loudly as he could.

"Bubbles," Junior said, rolling his eyes.

Beckett waited for the laughter to subside before saying something in Mrs. P.'s ear.

"It's a picture of what *looks* like bubbles," Mrs. P. said. "The caption says they're actually something called tennis courts. . . . He thinks the bubbly parts are meant to shelter them from the elements."

This drew more snickers, though not a rat among them knew what a tennis court was. Beckett spoke into Mrs. P.'s ear again.

"It's what they want to turn the pier into, he thinks," Mrs. P. told the crowd. "At the bottom of the notice it says, 'Beware, Rat Poison, Keep Out. Pier demolition commences August twenty-eighth.'"

This killed off the snickering. In fact, several rats started to moan. Mrs. P. was quick to reassure them, saying she'd heard of a time when humans tried to exterminate them before.

"No need to despair," she called out. "We're still alive. If need be, we can always go underground."

Her words comforted no one. This last remaining pier meant the world to the wharf rats: If they had to scuttle around in basements and sewers, they would no longer even *be* wharf rats. And before they had time to digest the idea of their precious home being demolished, Old Moberly's niece rushed out in tears. Her uncle, their beloved mayor, was dead. For everyone other than Augustus, who experienced a second thrill of excitement, the double whammy was too much to handle. A few rats stared at each other in silent shock, but most of them set up a keening and a wailing that shook the pier to its very pilings.

10

MIXED NUTS & MANCHEGO

THE NOISE EVEN WOKE PHOENIX IN THE FROMAG-erie. He'd been dreaming that he was perched between his parents near the top of their pine, enjoying the view of the shimmering ocean and wetlands and the rippling cornfield, so it was a rude shock to find himself alone in a dusky crate full of putrid cheese. But that wasn't the rudest shock. In his dream he was the old Phoenix, with his shiny fur and bushy tail—not a scabby, furless freak.

When the racket finally died down, he managed to drift off again. This time he was at Tyrone's funeral, with all the other squirrels sneaking him admiring glances.

But this dream was ruined too—by a growling sound. It was his stomach. He was starving. But he refused to be tempted by the whiff of nuts just detectable under the stink of the cheese. If he gave in, he would regain his strength and prolong this nightmare life.

Sometime around dawn a peculiar noise woke him again. Lifting his head, he could just make out a small rat on the other side of the crate. It was Oscar, poking holes in a wheel of cheddar with the sharp end of a pencil. Eventually Oscar started dropping tiny things into the holes, using the eraser end of the pencil to tamp them in. This seemed very odd, but it didn't keep Phoenix from drifting off again.

Next time he woke, Oscar was gone, and the nutty smell was stronger. On the outside of the can was a picture of the contents: nuts, all shelled, just like in the heaven mentioned by Tyrone's mother. He could almost taste them. And Beckett's admonition came back to him: Lucy had risked her life to get them. Even in his misery Phoenix could see there was something touching about that. Shouldn't he tell her about Oscar's suspicious behavior? She'd been so good to him, he probably owed her that much. Though to do it he would need a little strength. A nut or two. Just enough to tide him over till he could talk to her.

He struggled onto his hind feet, peered into the can, and nearly swooned. Not a single shell! He plucked out a nut. It was the first pecan he'd ever sampled, and the taste nearly made him swoon again. Next he tried a filbert. It wasn't quite as good, but still delicious. He ate another nut, and another, and another.

He had to force himself to stop. With a burp, he stumbled into the gallery. He stupidly glanced toward the compact mirror. But after the initial shock of seeing himself, he took a deep breath, walked back into the fromagerie, and started gnawing on the metal can. There was nothing to be done about his spoiled fur, but he might at least be able to do something about his farcical front teeth.

It took far longer than he'd expected, but after finally

working his teeth down, he went back out through the gallery, this time careful to avoid the mirror. In the parlor Mrs. P. was collapsed on her cushion, clutching her breakfast, a good-size chunk of cheddar. When he asked if she was all right, she groaned. He rushed to the front door and peered out. He'd been in the murky fromagerie so long that the early morning sunlight slanting in the dirty pier windows made him squint. Not many rats were out and about, though a group was gathered around four dead bodies lying near the metal drum.

As he emerged from Mrs. P.'s crate, he almost keeled over. Without his nice, bushy tail to wave behind him, his balance was totally off. He took a few more unsteady steps. It was as if he had to learn to walk from scratch.

His memory of being carried from Lucy and Beckett's crate in a shoe was hazy, but he knew theirs was a bottom crate. He also remembered that it was messy, so when he looked into one that was neat as a pin he wobbled on to the next. This one seemed right—full of books and periodicals—and as he crept inside, he made out Lucy and Beckett asleep in their shoes. He wasn't sorry to see that the father's shoe was empty.

Maybe it was because they were asleep, but the two

young rats didn't look quite as repulsive as when he'd first seen them coming down the ramp to the dock. Or maybe it was because they'd been nice to him. Either way, he gave Lucy a poke, and she sat up, blinking.

"Phoenix!" she said, surprised.

Beckett let out a sleepy moan. Phoenix apologized for waking them.

"It's just I think Mrs. P. is sick. And I saw something strange earlier."

When he told them about Oscar and the cheese, they both hopped out of bed and led him straight back to Mrs. P.'s. Mrs. P. was just as he'd left her. Her belly jiggled when Lucy shook her, but she didn't wake up. Beckett took the chunk of cheese from her paws and broke it in half, revealing an embedded green pellet.

"Get the antidote," Lucy said breathlessly.

Beckett suspected it was too late, but he went into the infirmary and brought back the canister he'd seen, along with a cup of water. Lucy shook Mrs. P. till she half opened her eyes. They tried to get her to take a capsule, but she mumbled that they mustn't waste them. When they tried to force it into her mouth, she turned her head away.

Lucy hurried back to the fromagerie, returning with a piece of manchego, Mrs. P.'s particular favorite. She shoved the capsule inside it and held the cheese under Mrs. P.'s snout. Mrs. P.'s whiskers quivered. Her lips parted. Lucy popped the cheese in. Mrs. P. chewed and swallowed.

Lucy and Beckett and Phoenix didn't leave Mrs. P.'s side, watching anxiously to see if the antidote would work. Beckett's pessimism grew as the day wore on, but Lucy kept her hopes up. As for Phoenix, he could hardly believe he cared about this oversize rat, yet he found himself wishing for her recovery. And just as the light in the parlor was beginning to wane, Mrs. P. came around.

"What are you all doing here?" she said, sitting up on her cushion.

"You were poisoned," Lucy told her, pointing at the evidence. When she explained what Phoenix had seen in the fromagerie, Mrs. P. didn't seem all that shocked.

"But I had cheddar for breakfast," Mrs. P. said, licking her lips. "I taste manchego."

"That's how Lucy got you to take the antidote," Beckett said.

"Ah. Clever girl."

"Phoenix deserves all the credit," said Lucy.

When Mrs. P. pulled Phoenix to her and gave him a hug, he was appalled and pleased at the same time. Though he was glad she was feeling better, who would want a hug from a rat? But then who would want to hug the hideous new him?

"You see, Beck, she's going to be fine," Lucy said. "You always look on the bleak side of things."

"If I'm not mistaken, Mrs. P. took Oscar in when he was a helpless ratling," Beckett said. "And how does he repay her? If that's not bleak, I'd like to know what is."

While Lucy was trying to come up with a response to this, Oscar himself came rushing through the doorway. He'd gone to hide under a stack of shipping pallets in the back corner of the pier, figuring he'd wait there till the poisoned cheese took effect. But he'd dozed off and had a nightmare in which he'd fallen into a vat of green pellets and couldn't claw his way out. Just as he was suffocating, he'd woken up and raced back here, guilt-stricken, to get Mrs. P. the antidote. At the sight of her looking fine, he froze, stupefied.

"I must be such a disappointment to you, Oscar,"

Mrs. P. said, rising from the cushion with a sigh. "I just live on and on, don't I?"

As she waddled over to him, Oscar cowered back, lifting a paw to protect himself. But all she did was open her amulet and hand him a small key that was inside it.

"For the lockbox," she said. "Take whatever you like. Heaven knows, you've earned it."

Oscar's yellow eyes widened. He'd been itching to get hold of this key, but now that he had it, it felt as if it were burning a hole in his paw. He dropped it and bolted out the door, nearly running into three rat elders on their way to call on Mrs. P.

"Dear me," said the eldest elder as Oscar sprinted away. "Why would he be in such a rush?"

"To look for more poison?" guessed the youngest, a graying female.

"But he doesn't have his sack," said the middle one, who had a matchbox in his paws.

The elders were something like judges, their chief duty being to settle disputes concerning crates, but today they'd come to ask Mrs. P. to assume the position of temporary mayor. They didn't have an easy time of it. They were considered old and wise by most wharf rats, but to Mrs. P. they were young whippersnappers. The matchbox they tried to present her was supposed to confer power and prestige—one of the mayor's traditional duties was to light the fire in the metal drum at the start of winter—but neither power nor prestige interested Mrs. P. in the least. Nor did she need matches. She kept a good supply of her own for lighting her kerosene stove and sterilizing needles.

"It would only be for a few days, till we can hold a special election," the eldest elder assured her.

Mrs. P. suggested they try the sergeant at arms, but they explained that Augustus would be busy campaigning, plus he didn't have her long experience, which seemed crucial in this emergency.

In the end she reluctantly gave in, so long as it was only for a short time. Before she could address the demolition situation, however, there was the matter of the four bodies to attend to. If rats died in the wintertime, the bodies were dumped in the metal drum and incinerated: cremated. In the summertime the deceased were given a burial at sea—or, at least, the bodies were dropped into the river, which generally flowed toward the sea. The logical place for this ritual would have been the half-submerged dock, but since young rats liked to swim there, the dead were slid under the front door and dropped off the south side of the pier. In the daytime this would have been in plain view of human joggers and bikers, so these burials were performed after dark.

By the time Mrs. P. squeezed out of her crate— followed by three elderly rats, two young rats, and a furless squirrel—night had indeed fallen. Except for Oscar, who'd vanished, and Mortimer, happily ensconced at Clancy's Pub, the whole rat community attended the pier-side burial ceremony. The moon had yet to rise, but the city's shimmering skyline gave them enough light to tell the corpses apart. One had been a cousin of Augustus's, and when the body plopped into the water, Augustus stretched to his full height and declared, "He is now, my fellow rats, in a far happier place."

"He's now fish food," Beckett remarked to his sister.

Another poisoning victim was a busybody who'd been known to scold Beckett for borrowing reading material from the fuel pile. When she plopped in, Beckett murmured, "Good riddance to the paper police." But even he was respectful when Old Moberly's turn came. Being the weightiest of the four, Old Moberly made the loudest plop. As soon as the river swallowed him up, his inconsolable widow rushed to the edge of the pier, bent on following him into the watery depths. But it was a very long drop, and when no one stepped up to pull her back from the brink, she contented herself with tossing in a scrap of black pantyhose she'd worn as a mourning veil. Phoenix, who'd known none of the deceased, found the whole thing quite pitiful. Creatures were supposed to return to the earth they came from. But in a place that was all concrete and pavement, he supposed a burial at sea was better than being left out to rot.

Not far from the drop-off spot was a huge, rusty cleat where transatlantic steamers once tied up. After the burials the elders basically pushed Mrs. P. up onto it so all would be able to see and hear her. Augustus thought it only fitting that the sergeant at arms join her, but before he could reach the cleat Mrs. P. called Lucy and Beckett and Phoenix up beside her for support, leaving no room. In fact, Phoenix would have gladly given Augustus his spot, and when a rat called out, "What's that mangy thing doing up there?" he tried to climb down. Mrs. P., however, grabbed his tail in her surprisingly strong grip, keeping him beside her.

When it suited her, Mrs. P. could make her voice almost as large as she was, and she did so now. "This mangy thing, as you call him, is named Phoenix," she boomed, "and he just saved my life."

Lucy gave Phoenix's paw a squeeze. He still wished he could disappear, though he did notice grateful looks on a lot of upturned faces. But then there was grumbling about Lucy and Beckett. The truth was, they weren't held in very high esteem by their peer group. Beckett's lack of athletic ability more than overshadowed his intelligence, and his whispery voice only made things worse. And even if Lucy was pretty and spirited enough to attract a top-tier rat like Junior, many couldn't see beyond her disreputable father and crummy crate.

The muttering prompted Mrs. P. to release Phoenix's tail and place a paw on Beckett's shoulder. "And thanks to this brilliant young rat," she said, using her other paw to point at the notice on the pier door, "we know the humans' plan. When is the demolition supposed to begin, Beckett?"

"August twenty-eighth," Beckett said.

"August twenty-eighth," Mrs. P. said, amplifying his answer. "Does anyone know today's date?"

No one had a clue, but Beckett was only too glad to hop down from the cleat and go find out. After he scurried away, someone in the crowd asked what "demolition" meant.

"It means they intend to tear the pier down, or at least our building," Mrs. P. said, "so they can put up their bubbles."

"How?" the rat asked.

"With machines, I imagine. That's how humans do most everything."

"But how can we stop them?" another rat wailed.

"That's what we're here to decide. Any ideas?"

"I'll turn them to mincemeat," Augustus proclaimed, drawing his sword.

The sword was actually a fancy toothpick meant for a cocktail, but Augustus brandished it in a swashbuckling way that roused the crowd. Mrs. P. complimented his noble sentiment.

"But I'm not sure one rat could stand up to them—even you."

"He can lead the rest of us!" Junior cried. "We'll form an army and attack them in their beds! And bite their paws. And their ugly snouts."

"Interesting idea," Mrs. P. said. "But I fear there are too many of them. Millions, I believe."

A young rat suggested they form a column across the front of the pier. "Then they'd have to run over us with their machines to do their demolition," she said.

"How lovely to be so young," said Mrs. P., keeping *and so naive* to herself. "I'm afraid there's nothing humans would enjoy more than running us over."

After this there was a long silence. Or not silence exactly. Rats talked among themselves in undertones—till there was a loud screech. Lucy's heart jumped. It sounded like a car on the West Side Highway slamming on its brakes. Could Beckett have been hit? The thought of her brother being taken from her made her so faint she had to lean on Mrs. P. for support.

But the crowd soon parted—and there her brother

was, dragging back the front page of a newspaper. It had come from the same newsstand where Oscar had filched the candy bar. Beckett hadn't been gone long, so it struck him as odd when Lucy hugged him as soon as he remounted the cleat. Once she let him go, he shrugged and smoothed out the front page for Mrs. P.

Mrs. P. had a vast knowledge of ailments and cures along with a remarkable memory and a fine palate for cheeses. But deciphering letters and numbers was beyond her.

"What does it mean?" she asked.

Beckett told her that it said August 25.

"It's August twenty-fifth," Mrs. P. repeated for the crowd's benefit. "That means we have . . ."

"Three days," Beckett said softly.

"Three days," Mrs. P. announced, "till the demolition begins."

"But the special election is in three days!" Augustus exclaimed.

This was news to most of them, since Augustus had decided this on his own. But no one questioned it except Mrs. P., who just suggested they might have to postpone it a day or two.

"There wouldn't be much point in electing a new mayor if there's no pier to be mayor of," she pointed out.

The words "no pier to be mayor of" had a baleful effect on the crowd. But the thought of having Beckett taken from her had given Lucy an idea.

"Yes, dearie?" said Mrs. P., seeing Lucy's raised paw.

"I was thinking," Lucy said. "To stop humans from taking something that means the world to us, maybe we could take something that means the world to them. As a warning. Like—if you do this to us, we'll do this to you."

"Logical," Mrs. P. said. "But what could we possibly take that they love?"

Lucy hadn't gotten that far in her thinking. Augustus realized the moment was tailor-made for a sound bite that would insure his election, but he couldn't come up with one. His son, however, waved a paw.

"They all wear those weird clothes," Junior said. "Maybe we could steal them."

"Steal their clothes," Mrs. P. said. "How would we do that?"

Junior had no idea.

"Maybe we could poison their food," someone chipped in. "My cousin Maurice could help us. He lives in the kitchen of one of their fancy restaurants."

"As I mentioned before," Mrs. P. said, "I'm afraid there are far too many of them."

The rats went on like this, throwing out one desperate idea after another, till finally Lucy raised her paw again and suggested they might need an outside perspective.

"What do you mean?" Mrs. P. said.

"Phoenix is from New Jersey," Lucy said. "Maybe he'd have an idea."

All eyes turned toward Phoenix. To his surprise, most of the rats looked more hopeful than repulsed—as if he might actually have an answer. He racked his brain. What meant the world to humans? He remembered his father taking him to their watering hole. The humans seemed to like swimming. But there was so much water around this city that he couldn't imagine how to keep them from it. What else did he know about them? He thought of Tyrone getting electrocuted and Great-Aunt Flo saying electricity was "vital to humans." The reason the two humans in shiny hats had climbed the tower

was to restore it. He looked out at the humans' glowing buildings, which put the few paltry stars in the sky to shame.

The rats were growing restless, but when he cleared his throat, most of them quieted down.

"One thing that means the world to humans is their electricity," Phoenix said.

"What's electricity?" someone asked.

"It has to do with elections," Augustus said knowledgeably. "They have them just like us. Very important."

"Actually, I think electricity may be what makes their light bulbs glow," Mrs. P. said.

As Augustus frowned, Beckett gave a start and turned to Lucy.

"Remember that building with no windows?" he said. "The flag had a light bulb on it, and three words: 'Con Ed Electrical.' And there were more words etched over the doorway. 'Consolidated Edison Substation.'"

Lucy repeated this louder for all to hear.

"Now *that's* interesting," Mrs. P. said.

"But what good does it do us?" Junior asked.

Augustus sniffed in agreement.

"Yeah, what good does it do us?" others echoed.

When it became clear that Mrs. P. had no answer for them, Augustus turned and started back toward the pier. No one could miss him, since he was the tallest of them all, and most of the rats followed his lead, many casting wistful looks up at the front of their beloved pier before slipping in under the door.

11

ALMOND JOY

As the assembly broke up, Lucy and Beckett and Phoenix helped Mrs. P. down from the cleat. Mrs. P. hadn't been this far from her crate since last summer, and on the way back she got a little unsteady, so her three young friends supported her till she collapsed on her favorite cushion. Phoenix then led Lucy and Beckett into the fromagerie, where he pointed out the tainted wheel of cheddar. Though a piece had been cut out of it, they were still able to roll it into the parlor and out the door. It didn't escape Lucy's notice that Phoenix turned his head away and tried not to breathe to escape the smell, and after they dumped the cheese off the dock, she pulled Beckett aside.

"Phoenix shouldn't have to stay in that fromagerie," she said. "Since Father's not home . . ."

Beckett approved the idea. But when they offered Phoenix the spare shoe in their crate to sleep in, he said nothing.

"Are you thinking about New Jersey?" Lucy asked, following his gaze to the lights across the river.

He was. The idea of sleeping in an old shoe had made him think of his comfy nest, just a few trees away from his parents. How he missed them! But even if he could find the bridge Mrs. P. had mentioned and cross it, how could he ever get all the way home? How could he negotiate that vast industrial area with the smokestacks? And if he somehow made it all the way back to his beloved woods, how could he show up looking like this? His parents wouldn't even recognize him. Giselle wouldn't nuzzle with him anymore—of that he was quite certain. So what was the point of returning? At the same time, why would he want to stay on this doomed pier with a bunch of rats?

As he was thinking he might have been better off sticking to his resolution to waste away and die, his stomach gave a loud growl.

"Er, is it okay if I bring the nuts over to your place?" he asked.

"You like them?" Lucy said, brightening. "I'm so glad."

Mrs. P. was snoring when Phoenix tiptoed in to get the nuts. He gobbled down a few, then put on the plastic top and rolled the can over to Lucy and Beckett's. It was getting late; they had already crawled into their shoes.

"Use that one," Beckett said, pointing at his father's.

Phoenix hesitated. The father's shoe didn't smell bad, but somehow the idea of it made him squeamish. Plus it looked like it would be a pretty tight squeeze.

Noticing his wavering, Beckett asked where he slept at home.

"In a hole in a tree," Phoenix said.

"On what?"

"My nest's mostly leaves."

Beckett got up and ripped apart a periodical he'd already read, fashioning a nest out of the paper shreds. When Phoenix tried it, he was amazed at how much it felt like home.

"Thanks," he said, snuggling in. "Thanks a lot!"

They were all tired, and it was nice and dark, yet none of them slept. Lucy was worried about the looming disaster, of course, but at the same time she felt strangely excited. They'd never had a houseguest before. After a while she whispered, "Anyone still awake?"

Beckett and Phoenix both grunted.

"That was so interesting, Phoenix," she said. "About humans and their electricity. Do you use electricity where you come from?"

"Not exactly," Phoenix said.

He told them about the pylons in the cornfield near his woods, and about Tyrone getting electrocuted.

"He shorted the grid," he said.

"Come again?" Beckett asked.

"He shorted the grid. All their lights went out."

"Maybe . . . maybe we could short the grid here?" Lucy said. "Imagine all those buildings at night with no lights!"

"The humans wouldn't like it," Beckett agreed. "But, it wouldn't do much good unless they knew we were responsible."

After a moment Lucy said: "What if you told them, Beck? We could take that notice off the door and you

141

could write on the back. Then we could tack it up again."

The idea of using Mrs. P.'s pen to compose an actual message appealed to Beckett. "But how would we get the notice off the door?" he asked.

"I've heard squirrels are good climbers," Lucy said suggestively.

Phoenix allowed that he might be able to do it. "But first wouldn't you have to figure out how to short the grid?" he said.

"How did your friend Tyrone do it?" Lucy asked.

"By touching two coils at once. But it got him killed."

"Would you recognize them if you saw two similar coils?" Beckett asked.

"I suppose."

"Then our first step would probably be to check out that substation."

"Oh, let's!" Lucy said. "But it's a big building. We'll need all the help we can get."

"We can round up a crew in the morning," Beckett said.

With that settled, Beckett soon dozed off. Lucy lay awake a while longer, wondering if Phoenix was still awake, thinking what a pity it was he'd fallen into their lives at such a perilous juncture. Phoenix was lying awake, too, wondering if *she* was still awake and thinking how dramatic life with these rats was. But eventually they both must have conked out, for suddenly it was morning.

As early as she thought acceptable, Lucy went to get Mrs. P. her breakfast cheddar and report on their plan. When she returned, Phoenix and her brother were up and about, but Beckett thought she should round up the scouting party on her own.

"We'd make lousy recruiters," he said. "I'm a wimp, and he's not even a rat."

Lucy insisted they go as a team, but Beckett may have had a point. They explained their plan to everyone they met, but they got no volunteers.

"Where's your beau?" Beckett finally asked. "He might help."

Junior was with his parents in their topmost crate, serving as a test audience along with his mother for his father's campaign speech. The speech was stirring, but when Junior tried to take off afterward, his mother corralled him into helping her hang a new postage stamp in the sitting room. It looked perfectly straight to him, but she kept insisting it was crooked. After adjusting it for her a dozen times, he threw his paws in the air.

"I have to go, Mum."

"Why?" Helen—such was his mother's name—could never understand wanting to leave their crate. It was such a showplace that she only left it under duress.

"It's broiling out," he said. "I want to take a swim."

"Just a whisker higher on the right," was Helen's response.

But he finally escaped—and soon proved Beckett right again. With Junior on their recruiting team they had no trouble rounding up a platoon for their mission. They couldn't head for the substation till nightfall, however, so Beckett crept off to practice his writing while most of the young rats followed Junior to the dock for an afternoon swim. It was so hot that even Phoenix went along, and he soon discovered that his insides hadn't changed as much as his outsides. When rats oohed and aahed over a dive Junior did from a piling, he felt just as annoyed as when squirrels had oohed and aahed over Tyrone's high-wire act. He figured that even if he wasn't as good a swimmer as the rats, he was a better climber, so he flailed out to a piling twice as high as Junior's—as it happened, the same one Martha, the pigeon, had landed on—and scrambled to the top. He had to close his eyes before jumping, but he surfaced to a rousing hand.

Now it was Junior's turn to feel aggravated, and later on, when they got ready to leave for the mission, he objected to Phoenix's coming along on the grounds that he might be a spy. This amused Phoenix, who had no stake in being part of the ratty expeditionary force. But it exasperated Lucy.

"He's the only one who knows what the coils look like, for goodness sake," she said.

With that, Lucy led them all out into the night. The jogging path was deserted, but the West Side Highway was a torrent of vehicles with glaring headlights. When they finally made it across, they slinked along single-file in the gutters and took detours to avoid sidewalk cafés.

A Con Ed truck was parked in front of the substation. Phoenix and the rats huddled underneath it, peering up at the building's floodlit facade. The substation had gone up in the lavish era of the great shipping lines, and the corners were embellished with ornate carvings. But the doors were closed, and the place looked impregnable as a fortress.

Around the side of the building, however, they found a ventilation grate just above street level. One by one they squeezed into a duct that led right into the power station. The place was enormous: brightly lit and pleasantly cool, housing three gigantic transformers that towered four or five stories high, each with a floor-level control panel manned by a human. Two other humans sat at a table, one eating a gyro, the other staring into a phone. None of them noticed the troop of rodents touring the premises. Lucy kept Phoenix up front with her, but he saw nothing resembling the two coils that had electrocuted Tyrone.

"Well, it was worth a try," she said when they got back to the duct.

"Where's Beckett?" Phoenix asked.

No one knew. Lucy frowned and suggested the rest of them wait while she retraced their steps. When she spotted her brother, partway up a tall spiral staircase in a back corner of the place, he gestured for her to come up. The risers were just short enough to be climbable. When she reached him, Beckett pointed to a diagram of the substation mounted under plexiglass on the wall. It indicated that there was another, smaller chamber above this one.

"What's that say?" Lucy asked, pointing at words written across the upper chamber.

"High voltage area," he said.

"What's that mean?"

Beckett didn't like to admit it, but he had no idea. Lucy looked up and saw that the spiral staircase rose all the way to the distant ceiling.

"Think that's the way?" she asked.

"Stands to reason. But it doesn't look like the stairs go through, does it?"

Knowing it would be too much for Beckett, Lucy went to check for herself. It was an exhausting climb, and at the top was a trapdoor that wouldn't budge.

On the descent she had to feel her way down each riser, hind feet first. By the time she reached her brother, she was totally frazzled. But Beckett had noticed something while she was gone.

"It shows an elevator," he said, pointing at the diagram.

They climbed the rest of the way down, and he led her to a metal trash can. Peeking around it, they could see gleaming elevator doors. Before long a human in blue coveralls walked up and pressed a button in the wall. The doors swooshed open. The human stepped into a chamber and set down a canvas tool sack he was carrying. The doors closed.

"Not promising," Beckett said. "They're unobservant, but even they would notice if we got in with them."

"Maybe we could use the elevator on our own," Lucy suggested.

"But how would we get to that button? The wall's too slick."

Remembering how Phoenix had climbed the tall piling beyond the dock, Lucy went back to fetch him. But Phoenix needed just one look to know that he could never reach the button unless they moved the trash can over to give him a leg up. Lucy dashed off again and returned with the whole squad. They all put their shoulders to the metal trash can while Beckett counted down from three. On "one," they all pushed. The can didn't move a bit.

They slumped back to the duct and made their way outside to the sidewalk, where it felt hot and sultry after the substation. Lucy led them to the front of the building and surveyed the facade.

"Maybe there's a way in from the outside, up near the top," she said. "Though it doesn't look like an easy climb."

"I got it," Junior said, marching over to the northwestern corner of the building.

Junior started making his way up the relief carving, which extended all the way to a cornice seven or eight stories up. It was late enough that the sidewalk was free of humans, so the rest of the party stood in a clump, watching. A rat named Emily, who'd been nursing a secret crush on Junior all summer, was sure she'd never seen anyone so agile. Phoenix, on the other hand, thought little of Junior's climbing technique. There was no natural agility, no lightness of footpad, no deft redistributions of weight. The rat seemed to be clawing his way up, grunting with the effort.

Sure enough, Junior didn't even reach the level of the streetlamps before his grunt turned to a shriek. When he hit the sidewalk, Emily rushed over and threw herself on him. She was a pretty rat but had a chip on her shoulder because, like everyone in her family, she was very petite—so petite that some suspected a touch of sewer rat. With Junior dead, however, her true feelings conquered her insecurities.

But rats are resilient creatures, and while the fall shook Junior up badly, it didn't actually kill him. The severest injury was to his pride—though he had to admit that it helped to have a pretty young rat draped over him, weeping.

When Emily felt him stir beneath her, she screeched with gratitude. "Thank goodness! You should never have tried it, Junior!"

Junior grunted with as much dignity as possible under the circumstances. "It's windy up there," he said, testing each limb before getting to his feet.

"But nobody could climb all that way!" Emily said, shooting Lucy an icy look.

As other rats agreed, Lucy looked suitably chastened. Phoenix felt a strange impulse to defend her. All she was doing was trying to save their home for them! He peered up at the limp Con Ed Electrical flag dangling high overhead and remarked that it didn't look windy to him. He stepped over to the corner of the building and started right up.

"It's too dangerous, Phoenix!" Lucy cried. "You're not fully recovered yet."

But in fact, awful as he looked in the compact mirror, his muscles were regaining their spring. His furless tail didn't make nearly as good a counterweight as his bushy one had, but he adjusted to it and felt a touch of pride as he passed the spot where Junior had lost his grip. Some of the building's relief work was actually quite deep, making for good paw holds, and there wasn't a breath of wind. Mainly he had to concentrate on not looking down.

When he reached the cornice, a gratifying cheer wafted up from below, but it was sadly premature. The cornice had two ledges. The lower one wasn't much of an obstacle, jutting out less than a squirrel-length, but the upper ledge stuck out three times as far. There was no way he could get past it without glue on his footpads.

Arggh! In his haste to show off his skills he hadn't given a thought to getting back down. How could he climb down backward with all those spectators? Of course, they were just rats. He shouldn't care what they thought of him. But he could just imagine Junior's scoffing and Lucy's disappointment.

Then something caught his eye: a surveillance camera mounted on the opposite side of the facade, just under the cornice's upper ledge. Maybe he could use it to get up. As he traversed the narrow ledge, he again missed his old tail, feeling like a tightrope walker without a pole. But he made it to the other side—and stretched a paw for the camera.

It was no good. The thing was out of reach. Disheartened, he started back. But in the middle of the lower ledge something else caught his eye. A support wire ran from the tip of the flagpole, which jutted straight out from the building just below him, to somewhere above the cornice.

Though it was only a short drop to the flagpole, gauging the jump meant looking down, and the sight of the upturned rat faces so far below gave him the willies. He tried to narrow his focus to the pole, telling himself that if he missed it, it would be a lot quicker way to go than a hunger strike. But he still procrastinated for a long time, heart thumping, before finally forcing himself off.

He landed safely, if not gracefully. After that, getting to the knob at the end of the pole should have been easy, but again, without his bushy tail, it was harrowing. And once he got there, he found that the reinforcing wire wasn't even as thick as the power cables over the cornfield back home. He gave the wire a twang. At least it was nice and taut. Feeling the rats' beady eyes all trained on him, he grabbed the wire—and his squirrel instincts magically kicked in. As he shinnied past the cornice, he felt a twinge in his bad shoulder, but Tyrone himself would have been proud of the way he zipped up the wire.

The wire was attached to an iron staple in the base

of a balustrade. There were gaps in the balustrade, and Phoenix squeezed through one onto a narrow balcony. The top part of the building was windowless too, but when he followed the balcony around a corner, he found a hole in the stonework: the end of a pipe used for electrical cables in the days before they were all buried. It led straight inside.

The upper chamber was smaller and dimmer than the lower chamber, and a lot hotter. There were circuits and conductors and crisscrossing wires everywhere, but, luckily, only one human: the man in the blue coveralls, bent over a circuit switch, his face flushed and sweaty as he adjusted something with a pair of pliers. And beyond him—aha!—a pair of humming coils that looked just like the ones that had killed Tyrone, only ten times bigger. Phoenix paused to think. Even if he'd been in a self-sacrificing mood, the coils were too far apart for him to touch at the same time. He looked around. On the floor behind the human was his canvas tool sack, with a promisingly long wrench poking out of it. Phoenix sneaked over and climbed onto the sack. But the wrench was too heavy to budge.

The human cursed and swiveled around. Phoenix

dove into the sack headfirst. As he squirmed between a hammer and a voltage tester, the human dropped in his pliers, and when they landed right on the still-tender part of Phoenix's tail, it was all he could do not to yelp. On the plus side there was an Almond Joy bar in the sack.

He'd finished half the Almond Joy when he heard receding footsteps. Poking his head out, he watched the human go into a closet near the elevator and come out with a pair of needle-nose pliers. The human didn't close the door, so once he was back at work on the circuit board, Phoenix went to check the closet himself. One side was devoted to brooms and mops and cleaning materials. The other side was all tools, including a level. The level looked long enough to make contact between the two coils, and it was light enough that Phoenix was able to push it gently out of the closet and hide it behind a bank of conductors.

With the human at work Phoenix figured he would have to come back tomorrow to try to short the grid, so he returned to the pipe and scooted out to the balcony. The cooler air felt nice, and sliding back down the wire to the flagpole was almost fun. But when he got back to the end of the cornice and sneaked a peak down, his heart sank. The rats were all still on the sidewalk, waiting and watching—leaving him in the same predicament as before. Climbing down the stonework headfirst would be too terrifying, while climbing down tail-first with all those beady eyes on him would be too humiliating.

He was stuck up there.

12

VERMONT CHEDDAR

WHILE PHOENIX WAS IN THE UPPER CHAMBER, Lucy had grown so agitated she'd unconsciously started chewing the tip of her tail. Beckett finally nudged her, and she immediately dropped her tail in embarrassment, but the tail chewing hadn't escaped Junior's notice. It made him wonder if his father, who didn't approve of Lucy, might not be right about her. Chewing your tail wasn't very ladylike. At the same time it aggravated him to think it had to do with her being so wrapped up in that mutant squirrel.

When the squirrel had been gone a long time, Junior

predicted that they would never see hide nor hair of him again.

"What makes you say that?" Lucy asked.

"I have a feeling he's been scamming us from the start," Junior said.

Beckett snorted. "Scamming us for what purpose?"

"Huh?" said Junior, putting a paw to an ear.

Whenever Beckett said something that annoyed him, Junior pretended he couldn't hear. It drove Lucy crazy.

"Why would Phoenix climb all that way if he wasn't trying to help us?" she asked.

"He likes to show off," Junior said.

"You saw him on the dock," Emily chimed in.

"Doing something well isn't necessarily showing off," Lucy pointed out.

Soon after this Phoenix reappeared on the flagpole high above them, and the rats let out a great cheer. Even Junior cheered. After all, the squirrel might have good news, and Junior loved the pier as much as anyone. He waited for Lucy's *I told you so* as Phoenix made his way to the end of the cornice, but she was too relieved to gloat.

It was a good thing she didn't, for after hesitating a while, Phoenix pattered back to the flagpole and pulled another vanishing act. Junior certainly wasn't above gloating, but he restrained himself in case Phoenix had just forgotten something. When Phoenix hadn't returned by midnight, however, Junior yawned extravagantly and said, "That squirrel's history. Time for some shut-eye."

"What do you mean, 'history'?" said Lucy, who'd been on the verge of chewing her tail again.

"He's ditched us."

"Why would he do that?"

"Why would he care about the pier? He's not one of us."

"But what if he went back for something and got hurt?" Lucy cried. "Or captured?"

Several rats nodded gravely, and Junior shut his snout. Lucy got more and more anxious. Finally, she blurted out that someone should go up and check. The rats liked the idea in principle, but no one felt like reenacting Junior's fall. When Lucy decided to attempt the climb herself, Beckett protested that she mustn't press her luck.

"You almost got killed rolling that can of peanuts," he reminded her.

"She did?" Junior said, frowning.

But Lucy wasn't to be dissuaded. As soon as she started up the building, Beckett rushed to an overflowing trash can on the street corner. The can was made of wire mesh, climbable even for him, and he tugged a discarded rag from the refuse, ignoring an interesting-looking magazine. Back at the foot of the building he got Junior and half a dozen other young rats to help him stretch the rag out directly below where Lucy was making her way up the relief work.

She'd already passed the spot where Junior had fallen. As a philosopher rat once said, "Fear is failure's best friend," and she wasn't a bit hampered by fear—though this may have been less because she was exceptionally brave than because she was too worried about Phoenix to spare any worry for herself. In any event her eyes were glued to the cornice as she worked her way up, pawhold by pawhold. But about halfway to the cornice her paws began to cramp from the strain. And then she had a stroke of bad luck— two strokes, actually. A gust of wind hit her, and at the same instant a car alarm went off down the block, startling her so badly she lost her grip.

"Pull!" Beckett croaked as Lucy plummeted.

He and the others pulled the rag so taut that when Lucy hit it, she actually bounced up in the air. After her second landing she lay on the rag, dazed, while they lowered her gently to the sidewalk.

"Are you all right, Luce?" Beckett asked.

"Not really," Lucy said, sitting up gingerly. "But thanks for catching me."

"Did you break something?" Junior asked.

She shook her head and looked up forlornly. There was still no sign of Phoenix on the flagpole or cornice.

"I guess all we can do is wait," she said resignedly.

A lot of rats lead nocturnal lives, liking darkness for their creeping and pilfering, but the wharf rats tended to sleep at night, and once the car alarm shut off, many in the scouting party started to yawn. While few of them bought Junior's theory that Phoenix had ditched them, there didn't seem to be anything they could do here, so they began trudging home. Eventually, Lucy and Beckett were the only ones left in front of the substation.

"Do you think he might have gotten electrocuted, like his friend Tyrone?" Lucy asked in a small voice.

Beckett had no answer. As he and Lucy took turns looking up, it got later and later, till finally there weren't even taxis cruising the neighborhood.

Finally, Beckett fell asleep on his paws. Lucy was exhausted too, and her neck hurt from craning, but she kept up her vigil till the front door of the substation swung open. As a human in blue coveralls came out carrying a tool sack, Lucy jerked Beckett off the curb, under the Con Ed truck. There was a beeping sound from overhead, then the human got into the truck, started the engine, and roared away, barely missing them with a rear tire. Beckett crouched in the gutter, trembling. Even Lucy was traumatized enough to agree that it was time to go home.

It was nearly sunup when they got back to their crate, and Beckett conked out as soon as his head hit the insole of his shoe. Lucy leaned back in hers, her eyes flicking between the empty loafer and the pile of magazine shreds. First their father had left them, and now Phoenix was gone too. She wasn't prone to tears, but a few leaked out before sleep finally carried her away.

While Lucy and Beckett slept in the next morning, the pier was a hive of activity. Junior and a lot of the other young rats were listening to his father's stump speech—or phonebook speech, seeing as Augustus was again standing on the phonebook by the metal drum. Even though the demolition was slated to begin the next day, he was more focused on the upcoming special election, for he had his doubts about Beckett's deciphering abilities and would have bet his prize ball of provolone that the notice on the pier door was just one of the humans' ubiquitous advertisements. But, if the humans *did* try anything, shouldn't the citizenry have a mayor who could stand up to them? As the rats waved their tails in approval, Augustus drew his toothpick and vowed that, if the humans dared show up, he would lead the charge against them.

Not far off, another crowd, this one composed mostly of older rats, was gathered around the three elders. The elders, less skeptical about the demolition, were encouraging everyone to make preparations for evacuating the pier.

"But where would we go?" someone cried.

"Underground, according to Mrs. P.," said the eldest elder.

"What's that, exactly?"

Wise as they were, the elders had no experience with this menacing-sounding place.

"Mrs. P.'s been there," said the youngest elder. "Maybe she can lead us."

The middle elder remained with the crowd while his two colleagues slipped off to pay Mrs. P. a visit. With Oscar gone and Lucy sleeping in, no one had gotten Mrs. P. her breakfast, but she still appeared in her doorway with a cheerful smile on her face. It disappeared, however, when the eldest elder told her the community hoped she would lead them underground.

"Oh, but I couldn't do that!" she exclaimed.

"Dear me. Why not?"

"Because I don't intend to evacuate."

"You don't believe young Beckett?"

"I have nothing but the greatest faith in Beckett's

reading skills. I'm just too old to pull up stakes at this point. They can demolish me along with the pier."

This was alarming. Since it was common knowledge that Mrs. P. was partial to Lucy, the two elders sought her out to see if she might be able to convince Mrs. P. to change her mind. Beckett answered the knock on their crate and told them his sister needed her sleep.

"But it's an emergency!" the youngest elder cried.

Lucy jolted awake. Normally, she would have been mortified to be found still in bed—and mortified for company to see their slovenly crate. But the memory of last night, of their dashed hopes and Phoenix vanishing, numbed her to embarrassment.

When the two elders explained why they'd come, she and Beckett followed them straight to Mrs. P.'s. The great rat invited everyone to take a cushion and asked the siblings how their mission had gone.

"Strange that Phoenix would come back out and then disappear again," Mrs. P. said after Lucy told her.

"I suspect something grisly happened to him," Beckett said.

"Poor squirrel," Mrs. P. said with a sigh. "But I suppose it's time for you to think about evacuating."

"We can't go without you!" Lucy cried.

"As I told them," Mrs. P. said, eyeing the elders, "I'm too old to—"

"No, you're not!" Lucy insisted. "Beckett and I can help you."

Mrs. P. shook her head. "Pack rats never part from their collections, dearie. And I have far too much to cart with me."

"But those are just *things*. Things aren't important."

"What a wise young rat you are," Mrs. P. said. "But remember, we're all made of time as well as fur and blood. We pack rats spend a lot of our time accumulating things, so they're part of us."

"We'll help you carry your favorites," Lucy said.

But nothing she could say could sway Mrs. P. When the two elders took the discouraging news back to the pallet, some rats went off to join Augustus's crowd. Most others adopted a wait-and-see attitude, packing up their valuables but holding off leaving till they had no choice.

Lucy and Beckett had the advantage of possessing no valuables to pack up. Beckett's library was public property—next winter's fuel. They also had the advantage of Lucy's knowledge of the city. And Beckett's ability to read would hold them in good stead in the world of humans. But they had no intention of leaving without making a final effort with Mrs. P.

When they stopped by her place, they found Mrs. P. stuck in the doorway between the gallery and the fromagerie. She'd gone to fetch some cheese for herself, but since the last time she'd done so, she'd put on quite a bit of weight. Lucy and Beckett yanked her back into the gallery by her tail. Undignified as this may have been, Mrs. P. laughed.

"Looks like I'll have to do a little gnawing on that door," she said. "Though if I'd been stuck long enough, I suppose I would have lost a few ounces and made it through."

Lucy helped her back to her cushion in the parlor, and Beckett brought her a chunk of her best Vermont cheddar. Lucy waited till Mrs. P. had a nibble before making her pitch.

"You can't really expect me to go down into the sewers when I can't even make it to the fromagerie," Mrs. P. said. "But you two must go." She set down her cheese, opened her amulet, and pulled out the key. "I'd like you both to have something nice to remember me by. Open my lockbox and take whatever you'd like."

The tears Lucy had shed in her shoe early that morning must have lowered her resistance, for a couple more leaked out now. She and Beckett politely declined the key. They stayed until Mrs. P. finally started yawning and shooed them out.

A lot of the older wharf rats had gathered near the metal drum, many with their bundled belongings stacked around them. Beckett tried to steer Lucy that way, but she headed for their crate, too distraught to face others just then, and he followed her. She sat down on the toe of her loafer and buried her head in her paws.

"Oh, Beck, I can't stand to leave her," she said with a sob.

"Shhh," Beckett said.

"What?" Lucy said, blinking up at him.

Beckett pointed at a scabby tail poking out of the nest of paper shreds.

"It appears the prodigal has returned," he said softly. "And he seems to be asleep."

13

TEPID COFFEE

As a rule, Lucy was no more of a screecher than a weeper, but a screech escaped her now. It was partly out of surprise, partly pure joy.

"Where've you been?" she cried, jumping up.

Phoenix, who'd fallen into a deep sleep after sneaking back into the pier, pawed at his eyes and blinked blearily. "I wish I could tell you," he said.

"But what happened at the substation? We saw you on the ledge, then you disappeared!"

"I thought of an easier way down."

This wasn't quite true. After shinnying up the flag-pole's support wire a second time, Phoenix had perched on the balcony in a quandary about his descent. Eventually, he made his way back through the pipe into the upper chamber, where the human was still sweating over the circuit switch. After some reconnoitering Phoenix located the trapdoor to the spiral staircase, but it was too heavy to budge. So he crouched by the elevator, figuring that was his best hope, and as he got hotter and hotter, he even felt a smidgen of gratitude for having lost so much fur. When the doors showed no sign whatever of opening on their own, he decided he would just have to wait for the rats to go home and then climb down the facade tail-first. But on his way back to the pipe, the human's canvas tool sack caught his eye.

"I got in and curled up in a corner of it," he told his two listeners.

His timing was perfect. After returning the needle-nosed pliers to the closet, the human picked up the sack and carried it to the elevator.

"What's it like, riding in an elevator?" Beckett asked curiously.

"It makes your stomach feel funny," Phoenix said.

The elevator came to a stop, the doors swooshed open, and the repairman walked out. When he stopped to talk to somebody, Phoenix climbed a hammer and poked his head out of the tool sack. They were in the lower chamber of the substation: He could even see the opening to the ventilation duct. But as he was about to jump, the human started walking again, knocking him back down into the sack. Jostling along, Phoenix heard a door open and close. More jostling, then a beep. Another door opened, and the sack landed hard on something. A door slammed. There was a wheeze and a roar. Phoenix tried to scramble up the hammer again but got jolted back down into the sack as they started to move. Then everything was herky-jerky.

When he finally managed to stick his head out for a look around, he got a shock almost as bad as when the hawk grabbed him. He was actually *inside* one of the humans' killing machines.

"I think you almost ran us over," Beckett commented.

"I wasn't driving," Phoenix pointed out.

The human drove for a very long time, though whether or not he managed to squash any creatures, Phoenix couldn't say. At last the human parked the truck, got out, and slammed the door, leaving the tool sack on the passenger seat. Phoenix climbed out of the sack and explored the cab of the truck. The windows were up. There was no way out. As the truck gradually filled with daylight, he huddled on the floorboard by the driver's side door, thinking he would zip out of the prison when the human came back. As he waited, his nose twitched.

"There was a bag of some twisty things under the seat," he said. "They were stale, but not bad."

"Pretzels?" Beckett guessed.

"Do pretzels make you thirsty?"

"I think so."

Luckily there was also some tepid coffee in a Styrofoam cup in a cupholder between the seats. After taking a slurp of this, Phoenix hopped to the dashboard and peered out the windshield. He didn't know it, but the truck was parked in the driveway of the Con Ed repairman's home, a semidetached house in Jamaica, Queens. They'd gone through a tunnel to get there. Another thing Phoenix didn't know was that the repairman worked the night shift and was now sound asleep in an upstairs bedroom.

As the sun rose higher, Phoenix heard rumbling noises and saw big silver birds slanting into the sky that reminded him of the one that had eaten Walter.

"Sounds like jet planes taking off," said Beckett.

"Who's Walter?" asked Lucy.

"The red-tailed hawk who brought me up here," Phoenix said. "I wonder how his eyases are doing without him."

Here was a word that stumped even Beckett.

"The hawk chicks," Phoenix explained.

Beckett wanted to know how to spell it. Lucy wanted to know if the eyases at least had a mother. Unable to answer either question, Phoenix returned to his story.

The repairman's truck grew hotter than the upper part of the substation. The coolest spot was under the seat, but even there it was stifling. Beckett and Lucy insisted it couldn't have been as hot as the pipe *they'd* been stuck in, and this may have been true, but Phoenix had been trapped in the truck far longer—all day in fact. He only survived by portioning out the coffee.

In the evening it began to cool off a little, but when the repairman finally opened the door and got in, Phoenix was too sapped and dehydrated to zip anywhere.

As the truck backed out of the driveway and pulled away, Phoenix just lay under the driver's seat like a squeezed-out sponge. Fortunately, the repairman turned on the air-conditioning, so by the time they passed through the tunnel into Manhattan, Phoenix had revived somewhat. Awhile later the repairman pulled up to a curb, turned off his truck, grabbed his tool sack, and climbed out. Phoenix *just* managed to hop onto the curb before the door slammed.

Again his luck was mixed. He was unlucky that they weren't back at the substation—the repairman had a job in an office tower in Midtown—but lucky that the building had a fountain in front of it. While the repairman went into the lobby, Phoenix climbed the fountain's marble rim and had a good, long slurp.

"Where was this building?" Lucy asked.

"No idea," Phoenix said.

"How'd you get back here?"

"Do you know what pigeons are?"

"Of course."

"I asked one the way to the river. Seems there are two rivers hereabouts, so I told him I wanted the one with New Jersey on the other side. He pointed the way.

Once I got there, all I had to do was head downtown."

Just as he'd fudged a bit about the beginning of his adventure, Phoenix fudged a bit about the end of it. In fact, when he got to the river, he remembered what Mrs. P. had said about the bridge to New Jersey being north. He sensed that he was north of the pier already, and he headed farther uptown along the edge of the jogging path. It was pretty much deserted at that time of night. After pattering along for a good while he saw what had to be the bridge. He climbed a lamppost for a better view. The bridge must have been a hundred times the size of the one that crossed the bay to the spit of beach houses back home. It was actually quite beautiful, a glimmering necklace stretched across the dark neck of water. But the swirling river reminded him how Lucy and Beckett had saved him from drowning in it. And it struck him that maybe he owed it to them to try to save their pier.

But in the end it wasn't this that made him climb down the lamppost and head south. It was the flickering image of Lucy in his mind. She was a rat, of course, like the one he'd seen rooting in the garbage back home. But there was something about her that made him want to see her again, if only to thank her and say a proper good-bye.

He didn't tell her this, of course.

"I'm so glad you're all right!" she said now. "Did you see anything that could help us? In the top part of the substation?"

"Any chance of shorting the grid?" Beckett added.

"Well, I saw two coils like the ones in the box on the tower back home," Phoenix told them. "But much bigger. And I found a piece of metal long enough to touch both coils at once. Of course, I have no idea if it would work."

"But it's worth a try, don't you think?" Lucy said, barely containing her excitement. "Could you climb up there again?"

Phoenix's left whiskers twitched. "I suppose so."

"Come with me!"

Tired as he was, he let her drag him out of the crate. He'd snuck into the pier earlier, so only now did the rats by the steel drum see him. They got quite excited, and Lucy stirred them up further by saying they might be smart to delay their departure. Then she tugged Phoenix under the sliding door and asked if he could reach the posted notice.

This was a piece of cake. The door was half-rotted wood, easy to sink his claws into, and it was a cinch to extract the tacks with his teeth. After the cardboard sign zigzagged to the ground, he stuck the tacks back into the door, then leaped down to help Lucy drag the notice back to her crate. They had to bend it slightly to fit it through the door.

"Your turn, Beck," Lucy said, flipping the notice to the blank underside. "Tell the humans they'll be sorry if they try to demolish the pier."

Beckett frowned. "Aren't we jumping the gun?"

"What's the good of shorting the grid if they don't know we're behind it? We're certainly not in any *worse* shape if Phoenix can't pull it off. They're already planning to turn this place into . . . what is it?"

"Tennis courts," Beckett said.

He eyed the piece of cardboard. At first nothing came, but when his sister thrust the pen into his paw, words began to flow. *Dear Humans,* he wrote. *Please quit putting out poison and leave our pier alone. We are peace-loving creatures but if you try to carry out your plan you will regret it.*

When he read his composition aloud, Lucy clapped

her paws. "Perfect! Don't you think so, Phoenix?"

Phoenix agreed.

"How shall I sign it?" Beckett asked.

Lucy wasn't sure, since it was doubtful the humans would know who "Beckett" was.

"Why don't you draw a picture of a rat?" Phoenix suggested.

This seemed a good solution. When Beckett drew a practice rat on the back of a magazine, he got another "Perfect!" from his sister. The one he drew under his message was even more convincing.

"Let's show Mrs. P.!" Lucy cried.

They found Mrs. P. dozing on her favorite cushion, but Lucy didn't hesitate to give her a shake.

"Ah, Phoenix, how nice to see you again," Mrs. P.

said cheerfully. "There was talk of you meeting with a calamity."

"He saw two coils in the top part of the substation!" Lucy blurted out. "Like the ones that shorted the grid where he comes from. Only bigger. And he found a piece of metal that could touch both at once!"

"Mercy," said Mrs. P., shimmying herself into a sitting position.

"Beck, read what you wrote," Lucy urged.

Beckett obliged.

"That seems to the point," Mrs. P. said when he'd finished. "I also like your rat."

"Thanks," Beckett said modestly.

"Phoenix is going to tack it up again so the humans can see it," Lucy said. "And if they touch our pier, he'll climb back to the top of the substation and put that piece of metal on the coils."

Mrs. P.'s broad brow furrowed. "I hope you won't short your own grid, Phoenix," she said.

As Phoenix promised to try not to, there was a knock on the crate. The eldest elder poked his head in the door.

"Er, excuse me," he said, "but we were wondering what's going on."

Mrs. P. may have refused to lead the wharf rats underground, but she'd agreed to be their interim mayor, so even though it was the middle of the night, she figured it was her duty to keep them informed. Once she'd squeezed through her door, Beckett and Phoenix each gave her a paw, and Lucy dragged the notice behind them. When they reached the congregation by the steel drum—hardly a rat was in bed on this ominous night—Mrs. P. told them that Phoenix had made it into the top of the substation.

"And," she said, "he's willing to go back again to try to disrupt the humans' electricity."

Phoenix held up his paws to quell the rats' excitement and advised them there was a good chance it wouldn't work. Beckett nodded in accord.

"Oh, but I know you can do it!" Lucy said. "I just wish we could all go up and help you."

Junior crossed his paws. "I don't see what good it'll do."

"That's where this young genius comes in," Mrs. P. said, smiling at Beckett. "He's composed a warning for the humans."

Beady eyes fixed on the notice, and when Lucy and

Phoenix dragged it under the sliding door, many rats followed while Beckett helped Mrs. P. back to her crate.

"Smell something?" Mrs. P. asked once she was sprawled on her cushion again.

Beckett sniffed and said, "Nothing good."

"I have a feeling it's coming from upstairs."

He'd never been upstairs, but he climbed the stirring stick now. There was a putrefying hot dog in a corner, but the upstairs apartment impressed him despite the stench. Oscar certainly hadn't done much decorating— the only furnishing was a bed made of rags—but there were two spacious crates with a handsome archway gnawed between them.

While Beckett was disposing of the hot dog in the storm sewer, Phoenix was putting the notice back up. It was tricky to hold it in place while extracting the tacks from the door with his teeth, all in the dark, but he had plenty of encouragement from below.

Once the notice was up, there wasn't really anything more for anyone to do that night. Other than Mrs. P., however, few got any sleep. Most of the rats milled anxiously by the front of the pier, waiting for the fateful day to dawn.

It finally did. The first joggers appeared, and the West Side Highway grew more and more congested. So did the river, with ferries and river taxis bringing office workers from New Jersey. But these things happened every weekday morning. As the sun climbed higher, the only unusual occurrence was a seagull flying in one of the pier building's broken windows. After circling twice under the rafters, it flew back out.

Gradually the rats' mood turned from anxious to cautiously optimistic. When there was no sign of a demolition team by noon, Augustus mounted the phonebook again to remind his fellow rats to vote tomorrow.

"If you're mayor, who'll be sergeant at arms?" a rat wanted to know.

"I'll appoint someone young and healthy," Augustus promised, looking pointedly at Junior.

Junior was stunned. He'd been thinking of rounding up the gang for some swimming and diving, only hesitating because Phoenix might come and show him up again. He'd never dreamed he was old enough to hold such an important position.

It didn't take him long to warm to the notion, however. And then things brightened even more as a weary

Phoenix crept off to the crate to catch a few winks.

"Let's hit the dock!" Junior said.

Lucy was about to join him when she noticed that Mrs. P. had appeared in her doorway. Lucy veered over there, and Mrs. P. showed her a vial of pills she'd put together for the rats to take along on their evacuation.

"Actually, it looks like we might not need to evacuate," Lucy told her. "There's no sign of the humans."

The words were barely out of her mouth when the pier began to tremble.

14

ROTTEN EGGS

Mrs. P. nearly dropped the vial.

"Earthquake?" she guessed.

Lucy didn't know what this meant, so Mrs. P. explained that it was when the earth got a little cough. She'd experienced one in her youth. But as the trembling intensified, Mrs. P. sensed this was more than a little cough and sent Lucy over to the pier door to investigate. Other rats were rushing there too, and they watched in alarm as three flatbed trucks drove onto the pier. One was carrying a bulldozer, another a backhoe, a third a dumpster. A pickup truck with a big spool of wire fencing in back pulled up as well, along with another pickup and a green van.

This green van was the cause of the demolition crew's late arrival. It belonged to an explosives expert named Neil Sullivan. Sully, as he was known, lived in Brooklyn, and if he had a job in Manhattan, he usually took the Battery Tunnel, as he had this morning. But the President of the United States happened to be in town that day to give an address at the United Nations, and as part of heightened security the police were doing random searches at bridges and tunnels. Sully's van was stopped, and he was arrested. He knew perfectly well that transporting explosives through city tunnels was illegal, but in twenty years he'd never been stopped, and he'd carelessly left a couple of blasting caps from his last job in the back of the van. When he got to the police precinct, he was allowed a phone call. He called the crew chief who'd hired him for the job. The crew chief called the real estate developer who'd hired *him* for the job. The developer, a rich and powerful man named P. J. Weeks, called his doubles tennis partner, the deputy mayor. The deputy mayor called the precinct, and Sully was released. All of which resulted in a six-hour delay.

The rats, who of course knew nothing of this, were

thrown into a turmoil—at least most of them. Back on the wobbly dock Junior and the gang frolicked away, oblivious, while Phoenix was sound asleep in his papery nest, and Beckett was so absorbed in an article in a *Scientific American* about a rat-maze experiment that he didn't notice the trembling.

Lucy dashed back to Mrs. P. to report that she'd been right about the humans and their machinery, then she dashed to her crate to tell Beckett he'd been right too, half dragging him to the pier door. They were just in time to see two humans approaching. Beckett couldn't resist poking his head out.

"Get a load of that!" said Sully, standing in front of the notice. "The rats are giving us a heads-up!"

"Some kid's idea of a joke," said the crew chief. "He ought to be in juvie."

"Maybe he'll learn some penmanship there," Sully said, laughing.

The crew chief sniggered.

"My son has to see this," Sully said, pulling his phone out of his pocket. "He's got a pet rat. White, with red eyes."

He took a photo, as did the crew chief.

"Got the dynamite you wanted," the crew chief said. "Kind of old school, isn't it?"

Sully shrugged. "Easier for a small job like this. Shouldn't take much to bring this old gal to her knees."

"Too late to do much today. Figure out where you want to put your charges, and we'll get things set up. We'll start work first thing in the AM."

"Give me a hand with this door, will you?"

Though Beckett was mastering their written language, he couldn't understand a word of the spoken variety, so he was as startled as the other rats when the door started sliding open. They sprinted for their crates, kicking up dust in every direction, and the first thing Sully did as he stepped inside was sneeze. He kept sneezing as he walked around checking support beams. But not even that was enough to wake Phoenix, so Lucy and Beckett finally dragged him from his nest. When he peered out of the crate, Phoenix was amazed to see the human inspector and the giant machines through the open pier door.

"Did the humans read your message?" he asked.

Beckett grunted. "But I don't think they put much stock in it."

Sully walked out of the pier building and came back a minute later pushing a handcart with a small trunk on it. After dumping the trunk, he wheeled the handcart back outside and put his shoulder to the door, sliding it shut with a forbidding creak.

Phoenix followed Lucy and Beckett over to the door to watch Sully climb into his green van and drive away. The flatbed trucks had already gone, leaving behind the bulldozer and backhoe and dumpster. The remaining humans were unspooling the wire fencing across the front of the pier area. Once the fence was up, they cut a gate in it, hung up a couple of signs, then piled into the pickups and drove away as well.

The rats started creeping out of hiding. First they checked out the ominous machinery looming outside, then they went back inside and gathered around the mysterious trunk. Augustus gave it a good sniff and declared that it contained rotten eggs.

"Why would they bring rotten eggs?" asked the youngest elder.

"To drive us out with the smell," Augustus suggested.

"I rather like it," the middle elder said, sniffing.

While other rats were weighing in on the smell, Beckett told them the trunk contained explosives, but with all the sniffing, no one heard him. Lucy hissed "shhhh" and asked Beckett to repeat himself.

"It says 'Danger Explosives' right there on the side," he said.

Since he'd been proven right about the notice on the door, the rats now took him more seriously. Many of them looked apprehensive, but Augustus looked downright shell-shocked.

"You mean they're going to blow us to bits?" he said.

"Stands to reason," said Beckett.

"Then what in the world are we doing here?"

So saying, Augustus sped out the back of the pier and returned moments later with his soaking-wet son, fresh off the dock. As he pulled his son toward the front of the pier, other wet young rats burst in through the back crack.

"Junior, where are you going?" cried Emily.

"Where are we going, Father?" Junior asked. "And what about Mom?"

"If anybody sees Helen," Augustus cried, "tell her we're down in Battery Park. I advise the rest of you to come too!" And with that he dragged his son under the sliding door.

In the wake of their departure, rats ran every which way, racing to gather up their belongings and follow him. As the pier descended into pandemonium, Mrs. P. squeezed out of her crate.

"Rats!" she boomed.

Rats stopped in place as if quick-frozen. Then, like metal chips drawn to a magnet, they migrated toward Mrs. P. As she had earlier on the cleat, she gathered Lucy and Beckett and Phoenix to her side.

"It's twilight," Mrs. P. said, checking the pier windows. "The humans are surely gone for the day, so let's not panic. Instead let's give these"—*young rats* was on the tip of her tongue when she remembered Phoenix wasn't a rat—"these youngsters one more chance to try to short the humans' grid and maybe change their minds."

All eyes fixed on Phoenix. Lucy grabbed his paw.

"Will you do it, Phoenix?" she asked.

"I can try," he said, his left whiskers twitching.

In desperate situations rats will clutch at the flimsiest of straws. Exchanging hopeful glances, many volunteered to go along to the substation. But Mrs. P. reminded them that such a mission called for ratlike stealth.

"You three go, since it's your brainchild," she said, indicating Lucy and Beckett and Phoenix. "But wait until dark."

"I could use a little more sleep," Phoenix admitted.

Back in the crate the sleep-deprived squirrel curled up in his papery nest, but even though Lucy and Beckett were very quiet—Beckett didn't even rustle a page—Phoenix couldn't drop off. He was suddenly feeling strangely alive, in a way he hadn't since rescuing Tyrone on the windy tower. When the light leaking into the crate began to fade, he abandoned the napping idea.

Quite a group followed the three of them out under the pier door into the night. Now that they were convinced of Beckett's reading ability, they wanted to know the meaning of the signs on the temporary fence. Beckett had little trouble deciphering them in the glow from the city lights.

"That one says 'Danger, Keep Out,'" he said, pointing. "And that one says, 'No Trespassing.'"

"Are we trespassing?" a very young rat asked.

"It's a matter of perspective," Beckett said.

The very young rat pretended he understood and joined the other rats in wishing the team good luck. Off they went. They reached the West Side Highway just as the signal turned red, so they scooted across. On the other side they moved haltingly through the gutters.

There were quite a few humans out and about, some walking dogs, some standing outside bars and restaurants smoking cigarettes, some sitting on stoops listening to music. On one block an open fire hydrant was flooding the gutter, so the trio had to mount the curb onto the sidewalk. As they hugged the base of an old apartment building, they got spritzed by dripping air-conditioners. The next building was a new high-rise, and Phoenix got a start when he spotted three rats on the other side of the tinted glass. Then it hit him that it was a reflection of them, and he was so chagrined he stopped in his tracks. He'd actually thought he was a *rat*.

"What's wrong?" Lucy and Beckett asked in unison.

Phoenix couldn't think what to say without insulting them, so he pretended he'd stubbed a paw in a sidewalk crack.

When they at last reached the substation, the whole area looked deserted, and they went straight to the corner of the building. Lucy gave Phoenix a hug. Beckett patted his shoulder and said, "Try not to get yourself fried."

It was another sultry, windless night, and the climb was easier than the first time, Phoenix's paws remembering the best niches. In short order he'd shinnied the support wire on the flagpole and was slithering through the pipe into the upper chamber. It was even hotter than last time, but luckily there were no humans around. He looked around anxiously for the level. Phew. It was right where he'd hidden it behind the conductors. He pushed it over to the two big coils, which seemed to be humming louder than before. If he stood between them on tiptoe and lifted the level over his head, he would just be able to set it down so it made contact with both coils. But if he did that, he realized, he might end up like Tyrone, and even though he'd just mistaken himself for a *rat,* he no longer felt like ending everything.

As he studied the problem, he wished Lucy and Beckett were there to help. Thinking of Beckett's parting advice, he fetched a sponge from the closet and placed it carefully on the edge of one of the coils. Nothing happened. He pressed the level over his head and carefully set one end of it on the sponge. He set the other end on the opposite coil. Nothing. He took a few deep breaths, then reached up and pulled the sponge away. The level fell and hit him on the head—*ouch!*—and clattered to the floor.

On the next try he followed the same steps, but before pulling away the sponge, he protected the lump forming on his skull with his other paw. This time the level landed on the not-quite-healed wound on his tail. Howling, he threw down the sponge and marched back to the pipe.

It was a little cooler out on the balcony. As the pain in his tail subsided, he glanced up and saw the moon poised between two glittering skyscrapers to the east. It looked just like one of Mrs. P.'s chunks of cheddar cheese. He thought about how Mrs. P. and Lucy had brought him back from the dead. And how Lucy and her brother were waiting expectantly down on the sidewalk.

He went back in through the pipe to give it one more try. He followed the same procedure, but when he pulled the sponge away this time, he snatched it like a magician snapping off a tablecloth without moving the silverware. The level dropped onto the coil with a resounding pop. Then came a sizzling sound, and everything went dark. For a moment Phoenix thought he'd actually done it—shorted the grid! But then the lights flickered back on.

Yet when he looked, the level was lying there touching both coils, which were no longer humming. He couldn't think what else he could do, so he went back out through the pipe onto the balcony. The moon was still poised between the two skyscrapers to the east. But it looked different somehow—brighter. He blinked, wondering if his eyes were playing tricks on him. No, the moon had definitely brightened.

Then it hit him why. The moon looked brighter because the skyscrapers framing it had gone dark. Not just them. Every building in sight was dark. Phoenix hopped atop the balustrade and made his way around the balcony. Everywhere he looked—east, west, north, and south—the whole city was as dark as his singed fur.

15

GRUYÈRE & PROVOLONE

"BECK?" LUCY CALLED OUT.

"Right here," Beckett said.

Rats have superior night vision, and Lucy quickly made out her brother leaning against the curbstone. They'd moved into the gutter when a human had come clattering down the sidewalk on a skateboard.

"Can you believe it?" Lucy said in hushed wonder.

Frankly, Beckett couldn't. He would have given very long odds against a solitary squirrel plunging a great metropolis into blackness. But well-informed as Beckett was, there was no way he could have known that the city's power grid had already been strained to the breaking point, what with the long heat wave and millions of air-conditioners running at full blast. The sudden loss of this critical substation had been the last straw.

Even the streetlamps were out. As Beckett's eyes adjusted to the feeble moonlight, he made out parked cars across the street, and the faint glitter of windows in the buildings beyond the cars. Then a taxi turned onto the block, and for a moment the headlights hit his sister's jubilant face.

In the distance people were shouting. Car horns were honking. It was almost as if the humans were celebrating the darkness too. But by the time another passing car's headlights lit things up, Lucy's face had turned anxious.

"Do you think Phoenix is okay?" she said.

"Let's hope," breathed Beckett.

They climbed back onto the sidewalk and looked up. Thanks to an emergency generator, lights had flickered back on inside the substation. But the outdoor floodlights weren't connected to it, so the facade was as dark as everything else in the neighborhood. Neither of them could make out the squirrel climbing tail-first down the corner of the building. But just as Phoenix was reaching the sidewalk, a garbage truck swung around the corner, catching him in its beams.

The two rats rushed over.

"You did it!" Lucy cried, giving him a massive hug.

"I wouldn't have believed it," Beckett said with something like awe in his voice.

Lucy insisted on hearing all the details then and there. Phoenix left out the part about the level hitting him on the head and tail but did his best to reproduce the popping and sizzling sounds.

He was telling them about sliding down the support wire in the dark when a pair of Con Ed vans came tearing around the corner and squealed to a stop. The three rodents cowered back against the building as humans jumped out and pounded up the substation's front steps. When the doors slammed behind them, Lucy said they had to go tell the others.

"They're not going to believe it!" she cried.

But the other wharf rats didn't need to be told. Most had remained out in front of the pier, too antsy to go to bed, and witnessed the plug being pulled on the city lights. Young rats danced in celebration. Older ones looked around hopefully at their beloved home. Junior's mother, Helen, who'd been toying with the idea of abandoning her beautiful crate and following her mate and son down to Battery Park, decided to stay put. Two of the elders raced back into the pier to wake Mrs. P. with the amazing news.

Mrs. P. accompanied them back outside to see for herself. "I have to admit, when I first saw that sorry-looking creature," she said, "I'd never have guessed he could pull off something like this."

"With the lights out, you can see the stars!" chirped one of several young rats who'd climbed onto the backhoe's shovel.

"You're right," said Mrs. P. She pointed. "That constellation over there is called the Great Rat."

"Maybe we should rename it the Great Squirrel!" cried another shovel-percher.

"Not a bad idea," Mrs. P. mused. "Though we mustn't forget that Lucy and Beckett played their parts."

The same young rats who'd grumbled when she brought Lucy and Beckett up onto the cleat now chanted their names along with the squirrel's. But when

the three failed to reappear, the chanting turned to wor-
rying. What if they'd sacrificed their lives at the substation? And another thing: the humans needed to be
reminded who had shorted the grid. If Beckett didn't
come back, they wouldn't be able to write any more
messages, and the whole enterprise would be in vain.

In fact, Lucy and Beckett and Phoenix were just on the
other side of the West Side Highway. But with no electricity the traffic signals weren't working, so the flow
of cars never quite stopped. They had to wait so long
that Phoenix's exhilaration from his adventure turned
to exhaustion, and he actually dozed off on his paws.
When a traffic cop finally arrived and halted the traffic,
Lucy had to shake Phoenix awake so they could scurry
across.

The heroes' welcome they received would have
been nicer for Phoenix if he hadn't been so dog-tired.
When the rats asked if there was anything in the world
he wanted, all he could do was yawn and say, "Well, I
could use a little snooze time."

Beckett echoed the yawn and the sentiment. At that
point even Lucy was flagging. But Mrs. P. wouldn't let

them retire just yet. Phoenix had to get the notice down from the pier door, Beckett had to fetch the pen, Lucy the box of matches.

When all three were back from their errands, Beckett crouched on the bill, pen in paw, and Mrs. P. struck a match. It fizzled out before Beckett wrote anything.

"Tell me when you're ready, dearie," Mrs. P. said.

Beckett thought. When he gave the nod, Mrs. P. struck a second match. Below his previous message Beckett scrawled: *We warned you!*

After tacking the notice back up on the door, Phoenix was finally able to drag himself off to his papery nest, with Beckett right behind him. As the other rats dispersed, Lucy started to help Mrs. P. home, but Mrs. P.

went no farther than just inside the pier door.

"I think I'll keep a watch on these machines," she said. "Be an angel and fetch my cushion, would you? And a smidge of cheddar?"

Lucy got her a cushion and a chunk of cheddar and sat with her awhile. "Do you think the power outage will stop them?" she asked.

"We can only hope," Mrs. P. said, breaking off a piece of cheese for Lucy. "But even if it doesn't, the three of you deserve a lot of credit. Now at least we have a fighting chance."

"It was all Phoenix. You should have seen him climb that building! And the wire at the end of the flagpole!"

"Wise of *you* to pull him out of the drink in the first place. But what's become of your admirer?"

"Junior? His father took him off to Battery Park so they wouldn't get blown up."

"Our sword-wielding sergeant at arms," Mrs. P. said wryly. "Have you noticed how the ones who feel the need to carry weapons are usually cowards at heart? But now off to bed. You must be dead on your paws."

When Lucy got back to the crate, Phoenix and Beckett were already sound asleep, and soon she was

too. They woke in the morning and joined most of the pier's older rats, who were gathered around Mrs. P. by the sliding door. Outside, the bulldozer's plow was glinting in the sun, but nothing else had changed since the middle of the night.

It wasn't long, however, before a pickup truck pulled up by the fence. With the power outage, most of the demolition crew, like most New Yorkers, were spending the day close to home. But there had been reports of looting and vandalism around the city, so the crew chief had decided to swing by to check the site. He came through the gate and walked around the machines. As he was about to head back to his pickup, the notice on the door caught his eye. He came over—and gawped. After a minute he pulled out his phone and had an animated conversation with his brother-in-law, who happened to be a journalist. Then he took another photo of the notice and sent it to him, along with the first one.

Once the human drove away, the consensus among the rats was that he'd taken Beckett's warning to heart. Most went back to their crates, Beckett and Phoenix included, but Lucy, who'd noticed that a lot of the young rats were missing, figured they'd gone for a swim and went to join them. However, the only creature anywhere around the half-submerged dock was a solitary gull on a piling.

When she got back to the crate, Beckett was too absorbed in an out-of-date *New Yorker* to care what had become of the younger set. But it wasn't long before one of the rats in question appeared in their doorway.

"Okay if we come in?" he asked.

Lucy was too flustered at the thought of guests seeing their crate to formulate a quick answer, so Beckett asked what they wanted. By way of answer the rat dragged in a copy of that day's *Daily News*.

"Where'd that come from?" asked Beckett, perking up.

"A deli," said the young rat. "They had all the papers."

"Um . . . would you mind if I look at it?"

"We got it for you."

"For *me*?" Beckett said, flabbergasted.

Another young rat came in with a plastic-wrapped slab of cheese for Lucy. Next came Emily, petite as she was, singlehandedly rolling a can of nuts for Phoenix. The young rats had gone on a foraging expedition. For many of them it had been their maiden voyage across the West Side Highway, but they'd reached it just as a policeman stopped the traffic. They'd been lucky in their choice of deli, too. The poor owner was so busy dealing with the melting ice cream in the freezer unit that the rats had the pick of the rest of the store. They hadn't grabbed goodies for themselves, however—only for Lucy and Beckett and Phoenix. The threesome grinned at each other, then at the others. They knew a peace offering when they saw one.

The cheese, a kind of Swiss called Gruyère, was unquestionably the best thing Lucy had ever tasted. Phoenix felt much the same about his offering: mixed nuts again, but this time *deluxe* mixed nuts. Beckett was so pleased with the newspaper that he gave in to the young rats' pleas to read it to them. Since there wasn't room for everyone in the cramped crate, Beckett took the paper out to Mrs. P., who was still by the pier door. As everyone gathered around, he started with the headline—BLACKOUT!—in white letters across an inky black front page. Then he turned to the article on page two and read:

"'Shortly before 11:00 last night a major power outage crippled all of Manhattan and parts of Queens and the Bronx. According to a Con Edison spokesperson, the long heat wave had severely overloaded the grid.'"

"What's a spokesperson?" someone asked.

"A person who speaks," Beckett said.

"I thought Phoenix made the lights go out," said someone else.

"He did," said Beckett. "They just don't know it yet."

"Keep going," said another.

Beckett read on:

"'The mayor is petitioning for state and federal assistance.'"

"What's federal?" someone asked.

Beckett had no clue, so he kept reading:

"'While Con Edison crews are working round the clock to restore power, the elderly and infirm are advised not to overexert themselves in the heat. There may be some relief in sight on that score. Thunderstorms are predicted for later today.'"

"Thunderstorms, cool!" said a young rat.

"Hey, Phoenix," said another. "After lunch, could you give us a climbing lesson?"

The inside of the sliding door soon became a climbing wall. Rats aren't built for climbing as squirrels are, so despite Phoenix's tips, there were a lot of tumbles. But the spectacle made Mrs. P. quiver with amusement, and most of the young rats enjoyed themselves too, bruises and all.

That night, slashes of lightning lit up the city's skyline, and rain splattered down through holes in the pier roof. When it was still raining in the morning, the younger set wanted more climbing lessons. This time Lucy joined in. Though Mrs. P. insisted the rats fetch the spare cushions from her parlor to make a softer landing place, Lucy didn't need them, being one of the few who never fell.

Beckett naturally avoided all this exertion, but when the sun finally broke through the clouds, around noon, he did go out to look for a newspaper. Junior and his father watched him leave the pier. They were huddled under the backhoe, shamefaced and drenched, having spent the pitch-black night under a dripping bench in Battery Park. Once Beckett crossed the jogging path, they crept out along the beam on the side of the pier, slunk in by the back crack, and climbed up to their crate. Helen let Junior slip in but blocked the doorway on Augustus, who scrabbled back down and burrowed into the fuel pile by the metal drum.

Junior dried himself off, spruced himself up, and broke a chunk off his father's prize ball of provolone cheese. But when he looked out the doorway and saw the climbing lesson, he lost his appetite. There was Lucy, her eyes glued to the mangy instructor. So were Emily's. Junior felt like chucking the provolone at Phoenix, but no doubt attacking the big hero would only add to his disgrace.

When Beckett came back with the paper, he looked almost excited, so the climbing lesson instantly broke up. Today's front-page headline was SMELL A RAT? Under it were two photos: one of the notice with Beckett's first message written on it: *Dear Humans, Please quit putting out poison and leave our pier alone. We are peace-loving creatures but if you try to carry out your plan you will regret it.* The other photo was of the notice with Beckett's added message: *We warned you!* The lead article began at the foot of the page.

"'Early this morning Con Edison restored service to neighborhoods in Queens and the Bronx and all of Manhattan above Thirty-fourth Street," Beckett read out in his soft voice, "but lower Manhattan remains without power. Yesterday we speculated that the outage was caused by an overloaded grid. However, a strange turn of events has come to our attention that may point the finger in a different direction. Preposterous as it may sound, this blackout, which has already caused New Yorkers untold misery and cost the city's economy untold billions, may be the work of rats.'"

The rats gaped at Beckett, then let out a hearty cheer.

"Maybe those humans aren't as dumb as they look," one of them said.

"What's 'preposterous'?" asked another.

"I think it means 'hard to believe,'" said Beckett.

"What's 'billions'?"

"A lot," said Mrs. P. "Go on, Beckett."

He kept reading:

"'The crux of the matter may well be a dilapidated west side pier slated to be turned into a new tennis facility. The demolition crew arrived there on Monday to find a message on a bill that had been posted earlier on the pier door (see top photo). The pier was already suspected to be infested with rats, but not surprisingly, the crew wrote off the message as a prank. That night: the blackout. Yesterday the crew chief returned to the site and found a postscript added to the message (see photo directly above). Of course, it may well be a hoax. To the best of our knowledge, rats are no more capable of writing messages than they are of causing citywide power outages.'"

This got a good laugh from the rats. Even Beckett chuckled as he turned the page. He lifted page two to show a grainy photo.

"Look familiar, Phoenix?" he asked with a mischievous grin.

The photo was of the level lying across the two coils

in the upper part of the substation. As rats chittered and clapped Phoenix on the back, Beckett read on:

"'The immediate cause of the blackout was the breakdown of an important Con Edison substation. And the cause of the breakdown was a piece of metal, a level, making contact with two high-voltage coils (see photo). According to a Con Ed spokesperson, no one at the station had been in proximity to these coils that evening, which leaves us with the mystery of how the level got there. Could the substation have been sabotaged by vigilante rats? "You can't be serious," said Mr. P. J. Weeks, the developer behind the pier project. The Con Ed spokesperson wasn't quite so dismissive. "Well, it doesn't seem very likely," she said. "But we can't rule out anything till we've gone through all our surveillance video." In the meantime, the substation remains offline, and lower Manhattan remains in the dark.'"

The rats stomped their paws and swished their tails triumphantly. Once the spontaneous celebration subsided, however, Mrs. P. felt compelled to warn them against letting their guard down.

"And I think we'd better open this little gift they left us," she said.

She led them over to the trunk of explosives. It was locked with a padlock, and the edges and lock were metal, but the sides were made of a composite material that looked more vulnerable. So Mrs. P. had all the younger rats smile and then proceeded to divide them into gnawing details. She exempted Lucy and Beckett and Phoenix, since they'd done so much for the cause already, but while Beckett went happily back to perusing the paper, Lucy joined one of the details anyway, as did Phoenix. He'd been eating only shelled nuts lately and needed to wear down his front teeth again. He also enjoyed the teamwork—and admired it. In fact, he was beginning to have a sneaking admiration for this whole pier community. He supposed Great-Aunt Flo played a role sort of like the elders, but in the woods there were no elections. They had no real leader, and if humans threatened to chop down all the trees, he was sure the squirrels would be too unorganized to do anything but scatter. Forming a united front against a common foe would be completely beyond them.

It took him and the other gnawers most of the afternoon, but they finally made a small puncture in the trunk. Once there was a hole, it was relatively easy to enlarge, and by dusk they had an opening that any of them other than Mrs. P. could have squeezed through. However, the trunk's contents blocked the way.

"Looks like candles," said Mrs. P, pulling one out.

It was red and waxy with letters stenciled on the side.

"'Dynamite,'" Beckett read. "The wick may be a fuse."

They emptied the trunk of twenty-four small sticks of the dynamite. The first idea was to dump all of them off the dock, but when a rat proposed using them to blow up the humans' machines, it was too tempting to pass up. They pushed two sticks of dynamite and the box of matches under the door. It was twilight now. The skyline to the north was lit up again, but their part of the city was still dark. After placing the dynamite under the bulldozer, between the shovel and the steel treads, young rats argued over who would get to light the fuse. Mrs. P. put an end to that. If anyone was going to get blown up, it would be her. She shooed them all away and did the honors herself.

After lighting both fuses, she dropped the match and waddled away as fast as she could. But the dynamite was only meant for weakening beams, and the blast wasn't much louder than a car backfiring. Mrs. P. felt the explosion in her old bones, but it didn't leave a scratch on the bulldozer.

The rats fell back on the original plan. Phoenix pitched in, helping Lucy drag one of the sticks out the pier's back crack. As the pile by the trunk dwindled, Mrs. P.'s pack-rat nature got the better of her. Her collection included candle stubs, but nothing like this. She surreptitiously settled her bulk over two of the sticks, like a hen on a pair of eggs.

The young rats were having a ball tossing the other sticks of dynamite into the river, so Mrs. P. would have been able to cart hers off to her gallery unseen if only Beckett hadn't remained with his paper. Though she admired his literacy, she wished he'd go read in his crate. But when she finally lost patience and carried her booty away, Beckett was so engrossed in an article in the Metro section—"Escaping the Rat Race," it was called—that he didn't even glance up.

16

SUNFLOWER SEEDS

MRS. P. DID NOT GO UNOBSERVED. Junior was watching from high up in his family crate. But he didn't venture down till late that night, after everyone else was in bed.

He wanted to practice some of the climbing moves he'd seen Phoenix demonstrate without anyone around to make fun of him. He started on the pile of shipping pallets where Oscar had hidden out, then moved on to the more challenging climbing wall.

But he didn't go unobserved either. As he took a third tumble from halfway up the door, his father emerged from the fuel pile.

"What's up, kiddo?" Augustus asked.

"Nothing," said Junior, not happy at being caught in a heap on the floor.

"Doesn't look like nothing to me. I've been watching. You're improving."

Junior got up and flicked the dust off his tail. "You think so?"

"Definitely."

Mollified, Junior explained that if someone was needed to climb the substation again he wanted to be the one. Augustus liked the sound of this. Since Helen had turned so frosty, he'd been thinking he might patter back down to Battery Park, where an attractive, if mustard-smeared, sewer rat had batted her eyes at him from under a hot-dog vendor—and where no one knew he'd deserted the pier like, well, a rat deserting a sinking ship. But an act of heroism on the part of his son might erase his disgrace. And was it even a disgrace? If he explained that he'd actually gone to Battery Park to look for help, it might seem like quite the reverse. So when things calmed down enough to hold the special election, he might still be the rat to beat.

He'd happened upon a bag of M&M's that Oscar had hidden in the fuel pile, and he parceled out a few to Junior to maintain his energy. Junior ended up pulling an all-nighter on the climbing wall, and with his father egging him on, he showed real progress. Finally, tuckered out, Junior dragged himself back up to the family crate. Augustus started to follow but thought better of it and retreated into the fuel pile.

Lucy rose at daybreak. She let Phoenix sleep on but stuck a piece of her Gruyère under Beckett's snout, hoping to lure him up to get the morning paper. Normally Beckett would have just rolled over in his shoe, but he was as curious about today's headline as she was, so he took the bribe.

The power must have come back on in their neighborhood overnight, for the traffic signals on the West Side Highway were working again. When Beckett got across, this was confirmed by the dripping air-conditioners. The newsstand was unusually busy, so he had to wait a long while behind a standpipe before making a dash for a paper, coming away with a front section.

By then humans were pouring out onto the sidewalks to walk their dogs or head for work, and by the time Beckett negotiated the obstacle course and got back to the pier, everyone was up and about, even Phoenix and Junior. Lucy fetched Mrs. P. from her crate to join the audience for the reading. Before starting, Beckett held up the front page for all to see. Lucy's heart lurched. Other rats sucked in their breath in admiration. The paper had gotten smudged on the journey, but there was no mistaking who was featured in the big, grainy photo.

Phoenix's first thought was: How in the world had they gotten that picture of him? Then he remembered the surveillance camera under the substation's cornice. It had caught him just as he was starting up the flagpole's support wire.

"What's it say?" Mrs. P. asked Beckett.

He read out the curious headline—RATS, SCHMATS!— and began the article:

"'The blackout ended shortly before midnight last night with power finally restored to lower Manhattan. The search for the cause may be over as well, thanks to an astonishing piece of surveillance video (see above) provided by a camera placed near the top of the substation. According to the time stamp, it was taken just minutes before the substation was crippled. The quality of the video is poor—it was night—but a zoologist brought in to inspect it claims the saboteur may be a new kind of mountaineering rat, one that has adapted to living among skyscrapers.'"

Beckett gave Phoenix a dry smile. Phoenix wasn't sure how he felt about "mountaineering rat," but several rats near him slapped him on the shoulder.

"'There is even a growing online movement,'" Beckett read on, "'in support of letting these tenacious rats keep their pier. We asked P. J. Weeks, the developer behind the pier renovation, if he thinks a few tennis courts are worth all this disruption to the city. "This story is one-hundred percent media-fabricated," Mr. Weeks declared. "You journalists should be ashamed of yourselves. As if rodents could be intelligent enough to bargain with us! You want my comment? Well, here it is: rats, schmats!"'"

Some rats hooted at this; others bumped paws. But, as at the last reading, Mrs. P. wasn't so sanguine.

"It sounds to me like the humans mean to resume their demolition," she said.

Beckett nodded grimly.

"Dear me," said the eldest elder, wringing his paws. "If they come back, how can we ever stop them?"

Everyone looked at Phoenix.

"Would you be willing to go up there again?" the elder asked.

Phoenix swished his still smarting tail, but seeing the hope in the rats' eyes, he could only say, "I suppose so."

Rats cheered. However, the instant Beckett opened his mouth to speak, the cheering stopped. It really was remarkable. Not long ago, Lucy and Mrs. P. were the only ones who'd paid the slightest attention to him.

"The humans won't be stupid enough to leave that level lying around again," Beckett predicted. "Or anything else you could use to cause a short."

"You're probably right," Phoenix agreed.

To everyone's surprise, it was Junior who spoke up next. "I know what we could do," he said.

Few rats had laid eyes on him since he'd decamped with his father, so there was a good bit of scoffing. But Junior lifted his chin and said, "I mean it. We could blow those coils with their own dynamite."

It was an excellent idea, except for one thing. "We

dumped all the dynamite in the river," Lucy said, groaning.

Junior turned his eyes on Mrs. P. For a moment she looked a little sheepish, but then she let out a good-natured laugh. "Well, I *did* stash a couple of sticks," she admitted. "In case of emergency."

Everyone agreed that the humans returning to demolish the pier constituted an emergency.

"But would the dynamite really work?" asked the eldest elder.

After mulling this over, Mrs. P. asked Beckett his opinion. Again there was an instantaneous, almost reverential silence.

"I've heard worse ideas," Beckett said.

Junior stood so tall he might have given his father, who was peeking out of the fuel pile, a run for his money.

"Of course, Phoenix would have to get the dynamite up there somehow," Beckett went on. "And we'd have to put up another message, so they'd know we're responsible."

"Phoenix, would you be a dear and get the notice down again?" Mrs. P. asked.

But before Phoenix could make a move, Junior

dashed under the door. With his new skills he had little trouble climbing up to the notice. Getting the tacks out was harder, but he managed that, too, dropping only one to the ground. The rats were suitably impressed when he dragged the notice back into the pier and presented it to Beckett.

Lucy got Beckett his pen. *Dear humans,* Beckett wrote. *Consider this your final warning. If you try to steal our pier we will steal your power again.*

After he signed it with another rat drawing, Junior took it outside and stuck it back up on the door. Most hoped that it would prove unnecessary, especially Phoenix, who didn't relish the idea of trying to blow up the coils. But at around midday three pickup trucks and the green van pulled up by the fence. The demolition crew filed through the gate, and Sully followed the crew chief over to the pier door. After reading the notice, the two men looked at each other in disbelief.

"Our 'final warning,'" the crew chief said. "This just gets crazier and crazier."

"I never thought I'd say this," Sully said, "but I'm starting to believe in these rats. I'll be darned if I'm going to set the charges."

"Not sure I blame you," the crew chief said, pulling out his phone.

He snapped another photo of the notice and sent it off to his brother-in-law. Then he made a call. It was very brief.

"Weeks doesn't sound happy," he reported.

"Not surprised," Sully said.

"He's going to honor us with a personal appearance. We can cool our heels till he gets here."

The rodents watched anxiously from under the door. A couple of the humans went back out through the gate and sat in one of the pickups listening to a ball game. The others leaned on the shady sides of the big machines, popping sunflower seeds into their mouths and competing to see who could spit them farthest.

The contest ended when a black town car pulled up beside Sully's van. A driver hustled out and opened the back door for a man in a beige summer suit with mirrored sunglasses and slicked-back hair that gleamed in the sun. Though Mr. P. J. Weeks looked quite a bit younger than the crew chief, the crew chief greeted him deferentially and ushered him over to the pier door.

"Hard to believe, isn't it, sir?" the crew chief said. "I'm thinking—once burned, twice shy."

"What do you mean by that?" Mr. Weeks snapped.

"Don't you think it would be taking a big risk to go ahead with the demolition?"

"You want to cave to this . . . this . . . *prank*?"

Before the crew chief could answer, a sweaty jogger who'd stopped by the fence answered for him, yelling, "Leave the rats alone!"

"Yeah, they need a place to live too!" yelled his running partner.

Mr. Weeks aimed a sneer their way. "Wackos," he said.

"So you don't believe the rats are behind this?" said the crew chief. "Even after that surveillance video?"

"Are you nuts? And even if they did mess with that substation, they could never do it again. Now let's get this show on the road."

The crew chief hesitated.

"Now! Or I'll find a crew that can finish the job!"

The crew chief swallowed his misgivings and told Sully to set his charges. As he and Sully slid the pier door open, the rats raced for their crates. Sully stepped inside and sneezed. Then he walked over to the trunk, pulled out his keyring, and used the smallest key on it to unlock the padlock.

Seconds later he stepped back outside, wearing a look of consternation. Mr. Weeks crossed his arms, clucking his tongue impatiently.

"What now?"

"They chewed a hole in the trunk, sir," Sully said. "All the . . . uh . . . explosives are gone."

This Mr. Weeks had to see for himself. Sully led him into the pier and showed him the empty trunk.

"How could they . . . ?" Mr. Weeks snatched off his sunglasses and looked around angrily. "Didn't we poison the vermin?"

"We put out more than the recommended amount," Sully said.

"Well, you'll just have to get some more dynamite."

"We could have it by morning."

Mr. Weeks cursed. He wasn't used to being thwarted. He jammed his sunglasses back on, stormed outside, and demanded the keys to the bulldozer.

"I'll knock the place down myself!" he bellowed.

He started the bulldozer and, after a couple of tries,

got it into gear. But when he released the clutch the bulldozer shot forward faster than he'd expected. The shovel
rammed into the front of the pier, and Mr. Weeks's
elbow smacked the steering wheel. Yelping and clutching his arm, he jumped off the machine and marched
back to his town car so fast his chauffeur barely had
time to open the door for him.

"First thing in the morning!" he shouted before
throwing himself into the back seat. "I want this place
GONE!"

17

M & M'S

AFTER THE TOWN CAR SPED OFF, THE BULLDOZER operator backed the bulldozer away from the pier while the rest of the crew had a good laugh. Sully and the crew chief consulted about explosives, then they all got into their vehicles and drove away.

But the bulldozer's crash had rattled the rats badly. As a rule they never left the pier in large groups during daylight hours, but now they all crept outside to inspect the damage, even Mrs. P.—and even Augustus, who stood at the back of the crowd. They stared up bleakly at the new gash in the siding. When the eldest elder asked Beckett if he could understand any of what the humans had said, Beckett shook his head.

"What do you think they're going to do?" another rat piped up.

That, Beckett could predict. "Nothing good," he said. "I'd bet my tail they'll be back with more explosives."

Many echoed his pessimism. But Lucy pointed out that, if not for Mrs. P., the pier would be blown up already.

"Very true," agreed the eldest elder. "Emptying that trunk showed remarkable foresight."

"As did stashing two sticks of dynamite," said the middle elder.

"We knew your experience would pay off," said the youngest one.

This was a bitter pill for Augustus. But his spirits lifted when his son volunteered to take the dynamite up to the top of the substation.

"I think maybe Phoenix should be the one to do that," Mrs. P. said as diplomatically as she could. "Lucy, dearie, would you give me a paw?"

They returned not five minutes later, Mrs. P. with a stick of dynamite, Lucy with the matchbox, and nine or ten rubber bands looped around her tail. When

Augustus saw that they intended to load Phoenix up instead of his son, he couldn't stay hidden any longer. He elbowed his way through the crowd, ignoring the sour looks he got.

"Not so fast," he said as he reached Mrs. P.

"Back from your little vacation?" she said.

"I went to look for reinforcements," Augustus said gruffly. "Didn't have much luck."

"Ah," Mrs. P. said, amused. "And now?"

Augustus stretched to his full height, eyeing Phoenix with distaste. "I just can't see why you'd want to give such an important job to a nonrat."

"Because it was Phoenix who got all the way up there in the first place," Mrs. P. said. "Plus, I hardly think of him as a nonrat anymore."

"Doesn't look like a rat to me. And how long have we known him? A few weeks? You've known my son all his life. Shouldn't he get preference?"

"It's not about favoritism, it's about getting the job done. Phoenix has been up there and knows the layout."

"Plus, Junior's a scuttler, not a climber," someone called out.

There were other protests, but they stopped when

Phoenix announced that it was fine by him if Junior went. He meant it too. Who would want to climb up to the steamy substation with explosives strapped to his back?

"Excellent," Augustus said, rubbing his paws together.

Mrs. P. was sure Phoenix was the one for the mission, but she couldn't force him to go. As Augustus placed the dynamite on Junior's back, Emily removed four rubber bands from Lucy's tail. Augustus used two of the rubber bands to secure the dynamite to Junior, one circling his chest, the other his belly, while Emily used the other two to secure the box of matches to the dynamite.

"Is it too heavy?" she asked.

"Nope," said Junior, checking to see if Lucy looked impressed.

But Lucy was more concerned about Mrs. P., who was suddenly looking worn out from all the unaccustomed activity. Lucy took one of Mrs. P.'s paws and guided her back into the pier. Beckett and Phoenix followed, collecting the scattered cushions and returning them to Mrs. P.'s parlor. Once Mrs. P. was ensconced on her favorite cushion, Lucy went into the infirmary to warm some broth.

But when she brought it out, Mrs. P. wasn't interested. Lucy looked at her brother in alarm, and Beckett hustled to the fromagerie for a hunk of manchego. This, Mrs. P. accepted. While she was nibbling, the youngest elder appeared at the parlor door.

"Er, they're waiting for you," she said.

"I'm afraid I'm not going anywhere," Mrs. P. said wearily.

"Not you, ma'am."

Beckett nudged his sister. "Junior wouldn't want you to miss his derring-do, Luce."

"You should go along too, Phoenix, as backup," Mrs. P. suggested.

Lucy and Phoenix traipsed after the elder but made a detour to their crate to grab a snack before the trip. While Lucy gnawed on her Gruyère, Phoenix broke into his new can of nuts. He ate a cashew and then pulled out a pale, round nut that was new to him. As soon as he bit into it, a wonderful aroma filled his nostrils.

"What's that?" Lucy said, sniffing.

Phoenix had no way of knowing it was a macadamia nut, but this didn't keep him from digging out another for her. And even if nuts aren't high on most rats' lists of favorite foods, Lucy found the macadamia nut enthrall-ing. Phoenix pawed through the contents of the can and found four more, so he and Lucy fortified themselves with two more apiece before heading off on their mission.

Beckett, who'd already dragged himself out that day for the paper, was happy to stay behind with Mrs. P. When he told her that she was finishing the last of the manchego, she sighed.

"I suppose I'll be out of cheddar, too, before long," Mrs. P. said wistfully. "Oscar may have been two-faced, but he was a good scrounger. Of course, my larder won't matter if . . ."

Her voice trailed off, but Beckett knew she meant *if the pier gets demolished and me along with it.*

"We'll restock your fromagerie," he said, to boost her spirits. "And get you whatever else you need."

This brought a smile to her face. "You know, I had an idea, Beckett—if by some miracle we do avoid disaster."

Beckett sat on a cushion facing hers. "What's that?"

"Lucy doesn't seem to much care for your crate—and here I am with two empty ones. Nothing would make me happier than if you moved in upstairs."

"Really? Phoenix, too?"

"Of course. If he sticks around. Do you like him?"

"Well . . . he's pleasantly quiet."

"I've been working on a pilatory for him."

Here was another word that stumped Beckett.

"Something to promote fur growth," she explained.

"I suspect he'd like that."

After finishing her cheese, Mrs. P. dozed off. Beckett tiptoed up the stirring stick. The upstairs was as luxurious as he remembered. Lucy would love it. The prospect of actually living there made him so curious about how things were going at the substation that he hustled back downstairs, tucked a handkerchief around Mrs. P., and took off to find out.

When he got to the substation, sunlight was streaming down the block from the west, turning the windowless facade honey-colored. A policewoman was standing guard on the front steps. The rats were gathered under a couple of parked cars, peering over the curb to watch Junior's progress up the corner of the building. Despite having a cargo, Junior was doing surprisingly well, having already well surpassed his first try.

Lucy and Phoenix were behind the front tire of one of the cars. Before Lucy could scold him for leaving

Mrs. P. alone, Beckett explained that she'd had a snack and fallen sound asleep. He also told them about her invitation.

"It's a palace up there," he said. "She wants you, too, Phoenix."

"Doesn't that sound wonderful, Phoenix?" Lucy exclaimed.

Phoenix smiled at the idea of a couple of those claustrophobic crates being a "palace."

Beckett squinted up at Junior. "Think he has a chance of pulling it off?"

The climber was halfway to the cornice. But while there was no wind, every time Junior looked to the west, the sun blinded him. And though at first the dynamite and matches hadn't been particularly burdensome, they seemed to get heavier every time he reached for a new pawhold. He looked up. There was still a dispiritingly long way to go. It seemed bitterly unfair that Phoenix had been able to do the climb unencumbered.

But just as he was getting the sinking feeling that he was going to have to turn back, Junior glanced down and spotted his father on the rear bumper of a red sedan, grinning like crazy and pointing at his chest. Why his chest? Junior peered down at his own chest and noticed two bumps under the nearer rubber band. He flicked out his tongue and snagged something: a green M&M. His father must have slipped it under the rubber band while loading him. The other M&M was yellow, and the two bursts of chocolate gave him a second wind. Upward he climbed.

But not even the combination of his father's encouragement and the chocolate could keep Junior's grip from weakening with every new notch in the stonework. He could feel the cargo pulling him down. And he was so high up! As he stretched for a next pawhold, his whole body started trembling. He was going to fall!

He looked down at his chest again—and this time nipped at the rubber band. The cinch snapped. The dynamite fell off him, giving him instant relief as it plummeted to the ground.

When the stick of dynamite and matchbox hit the sidewalk, the policewoman squinted in that direction, using a hand for a visor against the sun. As she headed toward the sound, Lucy vaulted up over the curb and made a dash to reach the dynamite first. After exchanging a quick look, Beckett and Phoenix dashed after her. Beckett grabbed the matchbox while Phoenix helped Lucy with the dynamite stick, each grasping one end. By the time the policewoman reached the corner, the sidewalk was bare except for some dried-up dog poop someone had neglected to clean up.

High above them Junior was still clinging to the building. But without his cargo it seemed pointless to try for the cornice, so he started back down. Having to feel blindly with his back paws made it very slow going, and even without the extra weight his muscles began to give out. He started trembling again. When he reached the spot he'd fallen from the first time, he lost his grip.

He landed on the sidewalk with the softest of thuds. The policewoman, who'd returned to the front steps, didn't even glance his way, so Lucy led a squad of rats over and carried him into the gutter, where he sat up woozily. His right side, the one he'd landed on, was throbbing from head to tail, but all he could think of was apologizing to his father for his failure. He struggled to his paws and took a few limping steps toward the red sedan. But there was no one on the rear bumper.

"Where's my father?" he asked.

The truth was, as soon as the stick of dynamite had hit the sidewalk, Augustus had jumped down off the bumper in disgust and headed back to Battery Park. All anyone could tell Junior, however, was that his father had left.

"I had no idea rats could climb like that," Phoenix exclaimed. "You nearly made it."

"I can't believe how far you got!" Emily gushed. "What's it like so high up?"

"All a waste," Junior muttered, eyeing the stick of dynamite miserably.

Of the three elders, only the youngest had managed the trek to the substation. She asked Phoenix if he would make the attempt.

"If the pier gets saved," Beckett said, giving Phoenix a nudge, "Mrs. P. might have a nice surprise for you."

"What's that?" Phoenix asked.

"A pilatory."

"A what?"

"Something to help your fur grow back."

In fact, the pleading look in Lucy's eyes had already persuaded Phoenix that he should go, but the idea of getting some of his fur back was an added incentive.

Junior watched unhappily as Lucy and Beckett cinched the dynamite and matchbox onto Phoenix's back with rubber bands. For a moment he was afraid Lucy was going to give Phoenix a kiss good luck. But, even if she'd intended to, she had no chance before the elder hissed, "The human's looking the other way! Go!"

Phoenix hoisted himself out of the gutter and scampered across the sidewalk to the southwest corner of the building. As he started up the stonework, Lucy grabbed Beckett's paw. Junior refused to watch—no way!—but soon found he couldn't help himself. In fact, every beady eye in the gutter was glued to Phoenix.

On his previous ascent Phoenix hadn't bothered to rest, but the added weight and broadsiding sun doubled the degree of difficulty. When he took a breather at about the spot where Junior had released his cargo, Junior found himself half hoping Phoenix would do likewise. But at the same time he didn't want to lose the pier. So he wasn't totally crushed to see Phoenix continue up. When Phoenix made it onto the lower ledge of the cornice, Lucy squeezed her brother's paw so tightly it was all Beckett could do not to squeal in pain.

Phoenix inched over to the middle of the building and focused hard on the flagpole, turning the distant sidewalk to a blur. The dynamite had shifted a bit to one side, so he readjusted it before making the short jump. He landed nicely, but halfway out the pole he stopped in alarm. Unless his eyes were deceiving him, the support wire was gone! He gave the surveillance camera a sidelong look. Drat! The humans must have removed the wire after seeing the video of him climbing it. Without the wire there was no way to the top.

He was surprised how devastated he felt. Somehow he'd gotten totally wrapped up in the fate of the rats' pier. But all he could do now was climb back down.

As he turned himself around, he heard a fluttering sound. A gust of breeze pushing at the flag, he figured.

But that wasn't it.

18

ROTTEN TOMATOES

WHEN LUCY SAW A BIG BIRD SWOOP OUT OF THE SKY and snatch Phoenix off the flagpole, she fell against her brother. Beckett wasn't much support. He almost fainted himself. As for the other rats, so many of them shrieked at the sight of their last chance being carried away that the policewoman heard them and made her way curiously toward the curb.

By the time she reached it, the rats were already scurrying off under the parked cars. Lucy was in such a state that she darted right out into the street without looking either way. It was sheer luck that there was no traffic at that moment and she wasn't flattened.

"He's still alive!" Lucy cried, seeing the bird flapping off toward the river with Phoenix wriggling in its talons. "Come on!"

She angled back to the gutter and raced toward the sinking sun so fast the bell around her neck tinkled and Beckett and the others could barely keep up. Her mad thought was that if Phoenix could squirm free of the bird's grasp, they might be able to catch him. But they encountered countless obstacles, for it was the time of day when humans were coming home from work. And even if the rats hadn't had to dodge taxis and hide under mailboxes, they would have been no match for the bird's speed. By the time they reached the West Side Highway, the bird was well out over the river, wheeling north.

The rats who'd remained behind in the pier were waiting anxiously just inside the sliding door. Even Helen, Junior's mother, had descended from her crate. All they needed was one look at the faces of the returning rats to know things hadn't gone well.

"What happened?" the eldest elder asked, wringing his paws.

Lucy didn't even break stride, running straight to the back of the pier, out the crack, and onto the dock. A traffic helicopter was hovering over the river, but there was no sign of the wretched bird. The view north up the Hudson was mostly blocked by the end of the next pier.

In her panic all Lucy could think to do was go to Mrs. P. The elderly rat was getting some much needed sleep, but Lucy gave her a violent shake, crying out that Phoenix had been snatched.

"What do you mean?" Mrs. P. said groggily.

"A bird grabbed him off the flagpole!"

Blinking, Mrs. P. sat bolt upright on her cushion. "What kind of bird?"

"A big one with claws!"

"Great heavens! He'd been through so much already."

"And he was only trying to help us! The bird carried him upriver, but I can't see where from the dock. I think he's still alive!"

Mrs. P. thought hard for a moment and said, "Do you know my old place?"

Lucy shook her head. Mrs. P. heaved herself up and got to the door quicker than Lucy had ever seen her.

"Highest crate in that stack," Mrs. P. said, pointing. "Up top there's a yardstick that reaches a hole in the roof. I used to go up when I wanted to get away from it all. You can see the whole river from there."

Lucy dashed away without even apologizing for waking her.

Normally, Beckett would never have considered climbing a tall stack of crates, but when he saw his sister doing just that, he followed her. The crates were offset, so it was nothing like scaling the substation: more like climbing a steep set of stairs. Still, by the time Beckett pulled himself onto the top of the stack, he was panting. Lucy was frantically trying to maneuver the end of a yardstick into a smallish hole in the roof. Beckett caught his breath and lent her a paw. As soon as the yardstick was in place, Lucy scampered up. Beckett followed, but he slipped off halfway up. It took him three tries before he made it onto the roof.

The view from up there was panoramic. You could see from the downtown skyscrapers to the ones in Midtown. To the south a regatta of sailboats raced by the Statue of Liberty. To the west, the sun was sinking over New Jersey. But Lucy stared north.

"See that dot?" she said, pointing.

Squinting, Beckett could just make out a tiny speck high above a barge. "Uh-oh," he said.

Moments later, the dot disappeared from view. Lucy gave him a despairing look. "What kind of bird was it?"

"An eagle or a hawk, most likely. Or maybe a falcon."

"What do they do to squirrels?"

Beckett winced. "Nothing good."

They sat there a long, long time, staring grimly upriver. The only birds they spotted were gulls. Eventually the sun ducked behind a tall apartment complex in New Jersey. The wispy cirrus clouds on the horizon turned amber and pink. In the pale blue higher up, two jets left crisscrossing contrails, taking Lucy back to the day they'd gone to the dock to watch another sunset. It seemed unspeakably cruel that tonight's was even more beautiful, since this time they had no chance of rescuing Phoenix.

Suddenly Beckett jumped up. "Look!" he croaked, pulling Lucy up as well. "Is that the bird?"

High overhead a large bird of prey was flapping north.

"Can't be," Lucy said, seeing that its talons were empty.

They sank back down on the roof. The sunset dimmed. The city brightened. Down below they heard rats bustling around, packing up last-minute items. Eventually, a gigantic ocean liner came steaming down the river. Beckett read out the name on the hull: BREAKAWAY. The *Breakaway* was all lit up, and when it came even with the pier, it totally blocked their view of New Jersey. It was so close they could hear the voices of the passengers leaning on the deck railings. They got a start when the passengers let out a communal gasp. The people were all pointing—right at them! Could the humans see them on the pier roof? But when Lucy glanced over her shoulder, she saw what the humans were really looking at.

"How?" she cried, scrambling back up.

The city had gone totally dark again! Beckett turned and stared at the blackened skyline in amazement.

"Maybe that bird brought Phoenix back or something," he said.

"That's ridiculous."

Nevertheless, they scurried off the roof and down the stack of crates. The floor of the pier was littered with bundles, but the rats were all gathered around Mrs. P., who was standing just outside her doorway.

"No sign of Phoenix?" she called as Lucy and Beckett came up.

"No—" Lucy began.

"But the humans' power is off again," Beckett interrupted.

"So I hear," Mrs. P. said. "It's bizarre. How do you think it happened?"

The rats fell silent to hear Beckett's theory. But all he said was, "It doesn't really matter."

"What do you mean?" Mrs. P. asked.

"Well, they read our warning. And now they've lost their power. They're bound to think we're responsible, even though we're not."

"There's something in that," Mrs. P. agreed. "I just wish we hadn't had to lose Phoenix."

Rats clucked their tongues tragically.

"We owe that poor squirrel," said the middle elder. "But should we evacuate or not?"

"It's unbearable, being so unsettled," said the eldest.

Junior's mother announced briskly that she was staying put, refusing to abandon her beautiful crate. Some rats felt the same; more leaned toward leaving to be safe. When the youngest elder asked Mrs. P.'s opinion, she advised waiting to see what tomorrow brought.

Comforted, if only temporarily, most of the rats drifted off to their crates, leaving their bundles out so they could make a quick getaway in the morning if necessary. Lucy and Beckett retreated to their crate too, but neither got much sleep. It was almost as if they'd traded natures. Lucy, usually the upbeat one, lay in her shoe conjuring up gruesome images of the things the bird of prey had done to Phoenix. Whereas for flickering moments Beckett actually let himself believe in his theory that the bird had brought Phoenix back to complete his mission.

First thing in the morning Beckett went out for the paper. The traffic was light, but when he got to the newsstand, the papers hadn't arrived yet. After a while a van pulled up, and three bundles of papers came flying out the back. Beckett let the humans who'd been milling around grab their papers first before creeping over and stealthily peeling off a front page. It was another hot day, so he used the paper as a parasol on his return trip.

As soon as he got back to the pier, rats streamed over to him. His sudden popularity still startled him, but he gamely held up the paper for all to see. The photo on the front page was so dark—it showed the lightless skyline against a night sky—that most of them had trouble deciphering it. He waited till Lucy arrived with Mrs. P. before lowering the paper to read the headline:

BLACKOUT: THE SEQUEL!

He flipped to page two and held up another photo. This one was of the notice with his message telling the humans it was their last chance. Rats chittered and slapped paws but calmed down when Beckett turned to the article.

"'At 8:40 last night the city suffered its second power outage in less than a week. But while the skyline went dark, we may not be in the dark as to the cause. When the demolition crew returned yesterday to what's come to be known throughout the five boroughs as the Rat Pier, they were greeted with a postscript to the message they found prior to the first blackout (see photo). So once again we are confronted with the incredible possibility that a citywide blackout was the work of rodents—literate rodents to boot!'"

During the reading rats were keeping watch under the sliding door, and just as Beckett was finishing the article, one of the lookouts cried, "Humans!" Everyone crowded over to look. Ten or twelve humans in street clothes had gathered on the other side of the fence. Two were carrying signs. Again the rats looked to Beckett.

One sign read: THE RATS NEED A PLACE TO LIVE! WE NEED OUR POWER! The other: LEAVE THE PIER TO THE RATS! BETTER THERE THAN IN OUR APARTMENTS!

"What are apartments?" a rat asked.

"They're like crates for humans, I think," Beckett guessed.

The signs were encouraging, and so were the rotten tomatoes the protestors lobbed at the heavy equipment. But ten minutes later a town car and a pickup pulled up. The crew chief got out of the pickup, and the driver of the town car opened the back door for Mr. Weeks. The protesters booed, especially when the crew chief pulled a box of dynamite out of the back of his truck. Mr. Weeks told them to get a life and led the crew chief through the gate.

"Where's that Sully?" Mr. Weeks fumed as the crew chief set the box down by the pier door. "I want these charges set. Every day's costing me money."

"He just texted me," the crew chief assured him. "He's close."

"I want the rest of the crew here too."

When the green van pulled up and Sully got out, the protestors booed, but Sully showed them a special edition of the paper he'd picked up, and that seemed to amuse them. It did *not* amuse Mr. Weeks. He demanded the paper, his face going an angry red as he scanned the front page. He crumpled the paper into a ball and threw it at the pier.

"Get this stuff out of here," he barked, stomping back to his car.

A protestor tossed one last tomato at the car as it sped away, and it splatted on the rear windshield. The crew chief frowned, made some calls, then gave a shrug and lugged the box back to his truck. Sully followed him out the gate. They exchanged a few words, then Sully drove off and the crew chief hopped into his truck. But instead of starting the engine he leaned his arm out the window and chatted with the protesters. Several of the protesters high-fived each other before straggling off with their signs.

Needless to say, the rats watched all this with intense interest. Soon another pickup arrived, and two members of the demolition crew got out and started ripping down the fencing. As they were piling it into the back of their pickup, three flatbed trucks pulled up. The crew chief supervised the loading of the bulldozer, the back-hoe, and the dumpster. It was a good thing this was a noisy operation or the humans would have heard the rats going wild. After the flatbed trucks drove the heavy equipment away, the crew chief walked up to the pier door and pulled off the notice, perhaps as a souvenir, and finally left.

Despite it being broad daylight, the rats flooded out of the pier. They could hardly believe their good fortune. The area was totally back to normal. The only evidence of the whole enterprise was the gash in the pier's siding.

Beckett located the crumpled paper and rolled it inside, everyone following him. He smoothed it out. The grainy photo on the front page was of Phoenix, with the dynamite and matchbox cinched to his back.

"Where was that taken?" Lucy gasped.

Beckett peered more closely at the photo. "Somewhere inside the substation, it looks like."

"But . . . that bird grabbed him before he got in," Junior said. "Are you sure it's him?"

Junior's fall had left an unsightly bump on the side of his head, and as everyone looked at him, he did his best to redirect their attention to the photo. It had been taken from above, and thanks to the dynamite you couldn't see much of Phoenix beyond his head and his tail. But this was more than enough for Lucy and Beckett to make a positive identification.

"That has to mean the bird didn't eat him!" Lucy cried.

"Thank heavens," Mrs. P. said quietly.

Beckett started reading the article, which told how the humans had installed a surveillance camera inside the upper chamber of the substation after the first blackout, and how it had captured the "perpetrator" moments before the second one.

"But if he caused the blackout, why hasn't he come back?" Junior asked. "It's been almost a day."

This, no one could answer.

"What does the headline say?" asked the youngest elder.

"Um, I'm not quite sure," Beckett said.

"Come on, Beck!" Lucy cried. "I know you can decipher it."

In fact, he already had. He just hadn't wanted to read it aloud. But the rats pressed him till he gave in. The headline was: SUICIDE BOMBER?

"What's a 'suicide bomber'?" a rat asked.

Beckett squirmed. "I'm not sure," he said at last.

But of course he knew, and by the aghast look on Lucy's face he could tell that she did too.

19

STALE PIZZA

IT'S TERRIFYING TO GET SNATCHED OFF A FLAGPOLE eight stories up, but when it happened to Phoenix, his terror was mixed with disbelief. Could he really have let it happen again? This time there was no cutting pain in his shoulder. The bird's talons hadn't pierced his flesh. But they gripped him too fiercely for him to squirm free.

The bird carried him over the tops of buildings, beyond the piers, and out over the river. After banking north, the bird quit flapping for a moment to inspect his catch, and they dipped down toward a Circle Line tour boat.

"What's on your back?" the bird asked as he flapped his great wings again.

"Explosives," Phoenix said.

"Explosives!"

"Well, nothing's going to explode unless I light the wick, and it's too windy up here to strike a match."

As soon as he said this, Phoenix realized it was probably a fatal mistake. A bird worried about getting blown up might drop him. It was a long way down to the river, but better that than being ripped apart by a hooked beak.

"Are you a marten?" the bird said.

"A marten?"

"Just a guess. Never seen one in the city anyway. I hope you're not a rat. I was looking for a treat for the missus. She's not partial to rat."

"I am a rat," Phoenix said—words he never thought he would utter. He twisted his head around and saw ruddy tail feathers. "Do you have a relative named Walter?"

"*What?*"

"It's just you sound like him."

"But I *am* Walter. You've heard of me?"

The bird gave a pleased flap of his powerful wings, lifting them higher. He'd always been secretly jealous of his famous cousin who lived by Central Park, and now it seemed that he, too, was a known entity! But when his prey identified himself as the squirrel he'd grabbed in Manahawkin, he felt a little deflated.

"What are the chances?" Walter said with a sigh. "I almost never hunt in the city, but I'd gone after a couple of starlings—and there you were, easy pickings."

Easy pickings! The words should be etched on his tombstone, Phoenix thought. Though the chances of him ending up with a marker seemed highly unlikely at the moment.

"But . . . I thought

you said you were a rat," Walter said. "You kind of look like one. What happened to you?"

"I landed in some hot tar."

"You mean when I dropped you?"

"Yup."

Far out ahead of them Walter could make out his destination: the cliffs of the Palisades, where his nest was. But directly below them was the bridge that connected Manhattan to New Jersey. He glided down and landed on the railing of the bridge's outer bike lane.

The landing was hard on Phoenix. For a moment he thought his backbone might be broken. But when the bird released him he managed to sit up dizzily on the railing.

"Good grief," Walter said, taking a good look at him.

"I know," Phoenix said ruefully.

"You saved my life—and look how I repaid you!"

"I saved your life?"

Walter shook out his wings and sucked a deep, whistling breath through his beak. "If you hadn't warned me, I would have gotten sucked into that jet's engines for sure. As it was, I lost three tail feathers. Quite a shock to the system. After I got home I didn't budge for a week."

Walter chuckled. "Though that had its plus side too. It finally got the kids out of the nest. All in all, I owe you a huge debt of gratitude."

Phoenix blinked, not at all sure he'd heard correctly. "Does that mean you're not going to eat me?"

"Eat you! If I were a night flier, I'd take you all the way back to Manahawkin."

Once Phoenix digested this miraculous offer, he gave a calculating squint at the setting sun. "Do you suppose it would be possible to fly me back where you grabbed me?"

"But of course!"

Moments later they were following the West Side Highway south. It was a scenic route, with the glittering city on their left and the sunset on their right, and under these new circumstances Phoenix could almost appreciate it. Walter was curious about the explosives, so Phoenix told him about his mission. This led to the rats and their pier problems.

"Which pier?" Walter asked, swinging left to avoid a helicopter. It wasn't a close call, but he wasn't taking any chances.

When they got closer to the pier, Phoenix pointed it

out. Walter said he'd once grabbed a pigeon off its roof.

"You eat pigeon?" Phoenix said, grimacing.

"In a pinch. But there aren't any there now, just a couple of rats."

Before Phoenix had a chance to see this for himself, Walter veered in among the buildings, gliding right between the arm of a crane and the top of a growing high-rise. As they approached the substation, Phoenix pointed out the balcony above the double cornice.

"There! Could you set me down there?"

This time, thanks to a lot of last-second flapping, Walter came in for a gentler landing. "I know it's rude to drop you and fly," he said, setting Phoenix upright on the balustrade railing. "But it really is getting dark."

"That's okay," Phoenix said. "I appreciate you not eating me."

After watching Walter flap away into the sunset, Phoenix hopped down onto the balcony and scurried around the corner. With the cargo on his back he had to squirm on his belly to squeeze through the pipe. The upper chamber was hot as ever. He crept over to the coils. They were humming away, just as they had before he shorted them out the other day. While he was gnawing at the rubber band around his chest to release the stick of dynamite, he heard a sound and froze. He wasn't alone. Looking cautiously around, he saw a guard sitting by the elevator, fanning himself with a magazine. Phoenix thought. He could still do this. He'd just have to be a lot quieter. So he lay on his side before continuing to gnaw through the rubber band. That way the dynamite wouldn't clunk when it fell on the floor. The band finally split apart, and the cargo came free. He slid the dynamite under the coils. Then the human stopped fanning himself, and Phoenix froze again. When the man went back to fanning, Phoenix struck a match. The stupid thing didn't light. He tried again. This time the match flared to life, but the sudden burst of heat reminded him so intensely of the hot tar that he dropped it.

The guard quit fanning himself again, and Phoenix returned to freeze mode. Only when the man went to use the restroom did Phoenix strike another match. Holding the flame as far from himself as possible, he lit the fuse. Then he dropped the match and sprinted for the pipe.

The dynamite exploded just as he stepped onto the balcony. The detonation wasn't all that powerful. The balcony didn't tremble under his paws or anything. Nevertheless, he watched one neighborhood after another blink out, till the entire city was dark again. The guard's cursing echoed out of the pipe. Yells and honks drifted up from the streets.

When Phoenix rounded the corner of the balcony, it didn't surprise him to see that the flagpole's support wire was still gone. There was no way to get down. But his predicament was softened considerably by the consolation of having accomplished his mission. In fact, as he crouched there looking out at the city he'd darkened, he felt a tickle of pride.

After the sunset's last gasp, it grew very dark, and he groped his way back to the pipe and into the substation. The emergency generator had kicked in, so the interior lights were on, showing five or six humans inspecting the damage. Phoenix crept up behind a metal toolbox for a better look. The dynamite may have had no effect on the bulldozer, but the coils were a twisted mess.

Two of the humans had on blue coveralls, and one of the two looked familiar. So did a canvas tool sack nearby. Phoenix dashed over to it. Climbing inside, he followed his own scent between a flashlight and a pair of Vise-Grips to a snug corner.

Though he had no intention of falling asleep, experiences like getting snatched off a flagpole by a hawk can be sapping, and he soon conked out. When he woke up, he felt hungry and well rested, but the canvas sack didn't seem to have moved. He peeped out. Four repairmen were hard at work, but the familiar one wasn't among them. Confused, Phoenix slipped out of the sack and crept over to the pipe and out to the balcony. The sun was almost directly overhead, which meant it must be the next day. Crawling back into the substation, he followed an interesting smell to the chair by the elevator and hopped onto it. An old, half-eaten slice of pizza was sitting on a greasy paper plate. He finished it off, even the crust, before returning to the tool sack.

In fact, the repairman had worked a night shift and left his tools behind, knowing he would be coming back. He returned that evening and put in another full shift. By that next morning the substation was still offline, but there was no more to be done till the new, custom-made coils were delivered. So this time he grabbed his tool sack, waking Phoenix from a light sleep, and took the elevator down to the lower level. Phoenix wasn't about to make the same mistake as last time. As soon as the canvas brightened, indicating they were outside, he pushed off the head of a hammer and hurled himself out of the sack.

He didn't make the most graceful landing. In fact, he hit the sidewalk snout-first. Nor did he escape the notice of the repairmen, who watched, open-mouthed, as he scrambled into the gutter. But the man didn't chase him, and at the end of the block Phoenix stopped under a parked minivan to rub his snout and catch his breath. Then he crossed the street and hurried toward the West Side Highway.

Like everything else, the signals on the West Side Highway were out, and while there was less traffic than usual, it never seemed to stop. The idea of dodging through the cars conjured up the image of the flattened raccoon on Hilliard Boulevard, and as he crouched on the curb, the blazing sun began to bother his burn scars. So he finally backtracked along the edge of the sidewalk and stopped in the shade of a fire hydrant.

Farther down the block Phoenix saw the owner of a steakhouse standing under his awning complaining to a passerby.

"No business! I'm losing my shirt! All my food's spoiling!"

This meant nothing to Phoenix, but while looking that way he spied a rat creeping out the open door of the restaurant with a bulging sack. The incensed owner didn't notice the rat dart across the awning's shadow into the gutter, but Phoenix recognized the rat instantly and scurried down the gutter to meet him.

"Hey, Oscar," he said when they were almost snout to snout. "What'd you get?"

"What's it to you?" Oscar said.

"Just curious."

In fact, Oscar was rather proud of his snatch. While the restaurant's chef had been transferring meat from the refrigerator to the meat locker, which would hold the cold longer, Oscar had managed to grab two medallions of beef. He opened his sack a tiny bit to give Phoenix a glimpse.

The medallions didn't tempt Phoenix in the least, but he complimented Oscar on his scavenging skills. "I'll bet you know this neighborhood like the back of your paw," he added.

Oscar grunted.

"Is there an alternate way across that highway?" Phoenix asked.

"Of course."

"Could you show me?"

"You wharf rats are too uppity for it."

"I'm not a wharf rat."

Oscar gave him an appraising look. "Guess you're not," he said, and he trotted off down the gutter with his sack.

As he followed, Phoenix stepped on a wad of gum and had to stop to scrape it off. When he looked up, Oscar was gone. Phoenix moved a little farther along and came to a drainage grate. Had Oscar disappeared down there? The subterranean world doesn't hold much appeal for squirrels, but then he heard a dreadful sound and looked over his shoulder to see a street sweeper coming right at him. It was either throw himself through the grate or get pulverized by the churning bristles.

He landed in a big concrete pipe right next to Oscar.

"Is this a sewer?" Phoenix asked, trying not to sound uppity.

"Storm sewer," Oscar said. He pointed west. "Pier's that way. Straight, left, right, then up."

Oscar dragged his sack off in the other direction. But after a few steps he stopped and looked back.

"Think you'll see Mrs. P.?" he asked.

"I imagine so," Phoenix said. After a silence he added, "Do you have a message for her?"

Oscar opened his sack and pulled out what looked like a waxy red puck.

"She likes these cheeses," he said, rolling it to Phoenix.

Phoenix picked it up, wishing he could read the label.

"She'll probably think I poisoned it, but I didn't," Oscar said.

"Why don't you give it to her yourself?" Phoenix suggested.

Oscar shook his head. He knew he'd done something so unforgivable he could never go back to the pier. Living in the sewers, however, had made him realize how cushy his former existence had been.

As Oscar dragged his sack away, Phoenix tucked the red disc under an arm and headed the other way down the pipe, walking alongside some water left over from the recent storm. After a while another pipe intersected the first, and he followed it to the left. This one was so dark he had to feel his way along. But when it intersected yet another pipe there was a faint glow off to his right. He scurried that way. It was tricky, climbing up through another grate without dropping the red disc, but he managed it.

He blinked in the brilliant sunshine. He was right in front of a dilapidated pier. But there was no fencing, no bulldozer, no backhoe, no dumpster. He shuffled closer. There was no notice posted on the door either. Yet the place looked familiar. He scanned the piers to the north and south. They'd all been fixed up, with corrugated steel siding instead of wood. He studied this one some more. It had to be the rats'. Except for a gash in the front, it looked exactly as it had when Martha first showed it to him.

20

MINI BABYBEL

A BUNCH OF YOUNG RATS WERE PLAYING IN THE front part of the pier, batting around a ball of wadded-up foil. One of them smacked it so hard it rolled out under the door. The others insisted she go after it. When she did, her eyes widened. She whirled around and ran back inside without the ball.

"He's back!" she cried.

The others fell over themselves racing to the door. At the sight of Phoenix they started yelling hysterically, and soon every rat in the pier came stumbling out to see what the commotion was. As Mrs. P. squeezed out of her crate, Lucy and Beckett hurried over to lend her a paw and joined the rear of the mob flooding toward the door. For a moment Beckett wondered if the uproar meant the demolition crew had come back. But the jubilant sounds coming from outside suggested otherwise, and when they walked out into the sunlight themselves, there were no humans around, just a big scrum of rats. At the sight of Mrs. P. rats moved aside, revealing the center of their attention.

"Land sakes alive!" Mrs. P. exclaimed.

Lucy blinked in astonishment. "Phoenix! You're alive!" Her voice began to quake. "I thought that horrid bird . . ."

Beckett tried to ask where Phoenix had been, but *his* voice was shaky too—even more strangled than usual— and hardly anyone heard. However, others wanted to know the same thing, so Phoenix let them in on the remarkable coincidence.

"You're never going to believe this, but it was the same hawk who brought me up here in the first place."

"But you said he was dead," Lucy said, wide-eyed.

"Turns out I was wrong."

"So the eyases didn't lose their father?"

"Seems not."

"But we saw him fly away with you!" said the youngest elder.

Other witnesses chimed in. Phoenix explained how Walter had stopped at the great bridge and then flown him back to the substation.

"Why would he do that?" Junior asked incredulously.

Phoenix shrugged. "Evidently I saved his life."

"So you were right, Beck," Lucy murmured, giving her brother an appreciative look.

Beckett cleared his throat. "Saving lives seems to be something you're good at, Phoenix," he said.

When Lucy repeated her brother's words loud enough for everyone to hear, there was a chorus of agreement.

"And you blew up the coils?" Junior said, impressed in spite of himself.

"Well, Mrs. P.'s stick of dynamite did that," Phoenix said.

"You're one for the books, dearie," said Mrs. P. "I thought I'd seen everything till you came along."

The middle elder asked Phoenix what he'd been up to since the lights went out, so he filled them in on his time in the tool sack. They filled him in on the demolition crew's surrender. A few joggers slowed down to look their way, but the Rat Pier had become so well-known that the sight of a horde of rats in front of it wasn't all that disturbing.

Beckett asked Phoenix about the waxy red puck.

"It's for Mrs. P.," Phoenix said, holding it out.

"Mini Babybel," Beckett said, reading the label.

"Oh, that's one of my favorites," Mrs. P. said. "That's so sweet of you, Phoenix."

"Actually, it's from Oscar. I just ran into him."

"Uh-oh," said Beckett. "Better toss it."

"I don't think he poisoned it," Phoenix said. "I think it's his way of apologizing."

After studying the offering thoughtfully, Mrs. P. tucked it under her arm. "Well, we seem to have weathered the storm," she said. "It's been a privilege to serve as your interim mayor, but it's been exhausting, so if you don't mind, I'll retire now."

Lucy gave her a paw, and the other rats sang them off with a rousing chorus of "For she's a jolly good pack rat!" Once Mrs. P. was settled on her cushion in her parlor, Lucy offered to get her a snack from the fromagerie, but Mrs. P. shook her head, eyeing the Mini Babybel in her lap.

"I do hope you move in, dearie," she said. "It's a little lonely here."

Lucy immediately went off to enlist Phoenix and her brother to help her move their things to Mrs. P.'s upstairs, but when she stepped back outside, Augustus was giving another stump speech—or cleat speech, since he'd climbed onto the cleat. When the latest blackout had hit, Augustus had given up hunting for his mustardy admirer in Battery Park and wound his way back to the pier, figuring there might be hope for it yet. He'd loitered in the shadows, and as soon as he'd heard Mrs. P. declare her intention to retire as interim mayor, he'd naturally sprung into action. He was now heaping praise on Phoenix, who was looking distinctly uncomfortable.

"Our debt to this resourceful squirrel is vaster than this mighty river," Augustus proclaimed, sweeping his sword from Phoenix to the Hudson. "I honestly thought our only chance would be to take up arms against the humans. That's why I went to Battery Park—to recruit reinforcements for the battle. But I had very little luck. The rats down there are a craven bunch, only interested in feeding and breeding. So I returned on my own, reckoning I would lead the charge when the time came. But no, this remarkable squirrel has spared me—spared all of us. If only he were a rat, I would nominate him to stand for mayor. As it is, it would be an honor to have him as my special advisor."

"How can he be your special advisor when you're not even mayor yet?" a rat asked.

Augustus covered his annoyance with a smile. "You make a good point. We must put the matter to a vote. No time like the present. We're all here."

Lucy raised a paw.

"Yes?" Augustus said.

"Mrs. P. isn't here," she pointed out.

Augustus wasn't overly fond of Lucy, and he was leery of Mrs. P., who had a disconcerting way of speaking her mind. But again he smiled his ready smile.

"And we owe her a deep debt of gratitude as well. But she's old—*extremely* old—and I fear her duties have worn her out. The humane thing to do, I think, is to let her rest. Any other objections to taking a vote?"

There was an edge to the way he said "objections" that daunted most of the crowd. But Phoenix lifted a paw. He was becoming more and more intrigued by wharf rat society, which seemed so much more developed than the tree squirrel society he came from.

"Yes, my friend?" Augustus said.

"I was just wondering. When you rats hold elections, don't you need more than one candidate?"

"Ah, you want to put yourself forward," said Augustus, making the common mistake of applying his own way of thinking to another. "As I said, were you only a rat, that would be—"

"*I* don't want to run for anything," Phoenix broke in. "I was just curious about your system."

"Ah. Well, often there is more than one candidate. Is there anyone who would like to nominate him or herself?"

There was an edge to the way Augustus said this, too, and again the only one to speak up was Phoenix.

"What about Beckett?" he suggested.

"A bright young rat indeed," Augustus said without missing a beat. "You and he could both be my special advisors."

"I mean, for mayor. Wouldn't it be advantageous to have one who can read and write?"

This was too much for Augustus, even from the savior of the pier. "A mayor has to be able to make himself heard," he snapped.

"Quite right," Beckett said. "I'm not the kind of rat who's cut out for public life."

"I think you'd make a fine mayor, Beck," Lucy said.

After their great triumph the wharf rats felt no qualms about lingering in front of the pier building in broad daylight—or even about making a racket arguing the merits of the two mayoral candidates. Beckett did his best to convince rats *not* to vote for him, but Lucy and Phoenix counteracted him, drumming up support by reminding everyone of the crucial role Beckett's messages had played in saving their home. Not liking the look of this, Augustus hopped down from the cleat and dragged Beckett back onto it with him, allowing the voters to see how dangerously young and pathetically scrawny Beckett was in comparison to him.

"Those in favor of me, Augustus, as your next mayor, please stand over here," Augustus said, sweeping his sword to his left—the safer side, nearer the pier door. With a slight downturn of his lips he pointed the other way. "Those in favor of the youngster, over there."

For quite a while few rats moved. Not many actually bought Augustus's story about trying to recruit rats in Battery Park, and the older ones found the idea of the lead candidate conducting the election most unorthodox. At the same time, while no one could deny that Beckett was one of their deliverers, Augustus certainly *looked* more mayoral. And Beckett was rather eccentric, to say the least. Most of the older rats began to drift to the right—Augustus's left—while most of the younger rats, the same ones who'd mocked Beckett the last time he'd been on the cleat, drifted to his side. The three elders, as was the custom, abstained, remaining in the middle.

"It appears to be quite close," the middle elder noted. "I see there are, um, five of you left undecided.

Now would be a good time to make a decision."

The five were an ancient rat with a cane, young Emily, Old Moberly's niece, and, perhaps surprisingly, Augustus's wife and son. The ancient rat was still sorting out the instructions, while Emily was waiting to see how Junior voted, and Old Moberly's niece couldn't stand to see her late uncle replaced by anyone. Junior was on the fence because he was still hurt by how his father had taken off after his failure at the substation, plus he didn't want to alienate Lucy by voting against her brother. As for his mother, Helen couldn't forgive her husband for leaving her behind the first time he absconded to Battery Park. But Augustus was giving her and Junior very meaningful looks, and in the end Junior knuckled under. Emily went with him, and in the end so did Helen, who figured she was too old at this point to find a new spouse. The old, deaf rat joined Lucy on Beckett's side, for Lucy had helped him up to his second-story crate on more than one occasion. Old Moberly's niece went for Beckett too, feeling that Augustus had pounced on the mayorship too quickly, before her uncle's body could even have drifted out to sea. The elders then took a head count. It was so close that they decided they'd better retally the votes.

As soon as Lucy had been counted a second time, she sprinted off into the pier and burst into Mrs. P.'s crate. Mrs. P. had fallen into a deep sleep—so deep that Lucy feared the Mini Babybel, which lay half-eaten in her lap, had been poisoned after all. But eventually Mrs. P. responded to Lucy's shaking.

"Why on earth would anyone vote for that deserter?" she said once Lucy explained the situation. "I'm all in for Beckett."

Lucy raced back just in time to hear the eldest elder declare that the confirmed result was a tie. She rushed over to him with her news.

"It seems we have an absentee ballot," the elder declared. "Beckett wins by one!"

Up on the cleat Augustus looked as if he'd choked on a piece of moldy cheese. "Another recount!" he croaked.

The elders shook their heads in unison. One recount was the limit.

"But . . ." Augustus looked around desperately. "But the candidates haven't voted yet! We're allowed to vote."

"True enough," the eldest elder said. "But it would hardly change the outcome."

This didn't keep Augustus from hopping down to join his supporters. Lucy called out, "Come on, Beck!" but when Beckett climbed clumsily down from the cleat he joined Augustus's side. This provoked cries of outrage from Lucy and the rest of her brother's backers, but the truth was, Beckett was worried about sacrificing reading time for administrative duties.

Augustus clasped Beckett as if he were a second son. "Well now, I believe that settles it," Augustus said when the furor died down. "I win by one vote."

None of the elders could contradict him. Nor could Phoenix or Lucy, dismayed as they were. Augustus remounted the cleat and drew his sword again, thinking he would present it to his son as the new sergeant at arms, thereby cementing an Augustan dynasty. But before he could call Junior up, a strange metallic sound caused everyone to look around.

"Father!" Lucy cried.

Indeed, it was Mortimer, rolling an unopened can of New Amsterdam ale in their direction. The latest power outage had knocked out Clancy's air-conditioning for the second time, and the place had become so stifling that Mortimer had decided to head back to the pier, where there might be the occasional breeze off the river. Rolling the heavy can was hard work, so as he neared the crowd, he wasn't sorry for a rest.

"Who died?" he asked once the can came to a stop. It seemed early in the day for a burial service, but he couldn't think of any other explanation for all the rats being out here.

"No one," said the eldest elder. "We've been electing a new mayor."

"Your son lost by a whisker," said the middle elder.

"Beckett?" Mortimer said, genuinely surprised. "You're pulling my tail."

The youngest elder shook her head. "He may be soft-spoken, but he fell only one vote short. His own, as it happens."

Mortimer had a thick hide, but "soft-spoken" got to him. When he'd throttled Beckett for rustling pages, he'd had a terrible hangover, but he hadn't forgotten the incident. Nor had he forgotten Augustus's bragging and bullying from the days of their youth. And when he squinted from the blowhard on the cleat to his son, he got a little shock. The full sunlight revealed something he'd never noticed before: that Beckett had Arabella's eyes and chin.

"You don't mean to tell me you fell for that imposter?" he said, waving a contemptuous paw at Augustus.

"We've elected our former sergeant at arms, if that's what you mean," said the eldest elder.

"Fiddlesticks," Mortimer said. "I vote for Beckett."

This caused quite a hubbub. While Beckett looked floored, even aghast, his backers whooped and slapped paws, and Lucy skirted the beer can to give her father a hug. A few of Augustus's backers hissed, and Augustus himself declared indignantly that the polls had already closed. After a consultation the elders disagreed, whereupon Augustus argued that Mortimer didn't even live on the pier anymore, so his vote shouldn't count.

"I've lived here my whole life," Mortimer said. "If spending a night or two off-pier disqualifies you, then I'm afraid your vote wouldn't count either, Augie."

Augustus detested that nickname, but he couldn't contest Mortimer's point. "In that case," he said, "a tie surely goes to the older candidate."

The elders consulted again, and again they disappointed Augustus, declaring there was no such custom. When they asked Beckett to rejoin Augustus on the cleat, Phoenix and Lucy pushed the reluctant candidate up onto it.

"In the case of a tie, voters are given a final chance to change their minds," proclaimed the eldest elder. "If anyone is so inclined, now is definitely the time."

21

MACADAMIA NUT

THE VOTERS STARTED CHITTERING AMONG THEM-
selves, making so much noise that none of them heard
the flapping sound overhead. But Phoenix did. Unlike
the rats, he'd been lectured his whole life about watching out for birds of prey, and though he hadn't done a
very good job of it, his two lapses had at least taught
him something. Unfortunately, he had nowhere to duck
for cover. Hordes of rats hemmed him in on his left and
right, while in front of him was a big cleat, and behind
him, a beer can.

In another instant the rats heard the wing beats
too, and looked up to see a huge hawk descending on

them. Most froze in terror—but not the two mayoral candidates. Augustus dropped his sword with a surprisingly high-pitched shriek, leaped off the cleat, raced right around his constituents, and dove under the pier door. Beckett jumped off the cleat and threw himself over his sister to shield her from the bird's talons.

But the talons didn't grab him or Lucy or anyone else. With a great flapping of wings the bird settled on the vacated cleat. At that point most of the rats had recovered from their shock enough to start rushing toward the pier, and in the melee the eldest elder got knocked over. As his two fellow elders dragged him toward the pier door, Phoenix called out: "Don't worry! He's a friend of mine!"

This had little effect on the fleeing rats. Phoenix gave a shrug and turned to the bird, the very red-tailed hawk who'd grabbed him twice in the past.

"Morning, Walter," he said.

"Morning, Phoenix," said Walter, rearranging his tail feathers so the missing ones were less noticeable.

In his rush to protect Lucy, Beckett had knocked her over, and they lay tangled on the ground, while their father was pressed flat behind his beer can.

"These are friends of mine," Phoenix said as the three got shakily to their paws. "Lucy, and Beckett, and their father, Mortimer."

"Nice to meet you, rats," Walter said with a slight inclination of his head.

None of the three said a word. Face-to-face with a hawk, even Mortimer was struck dumb.

"You really never cease to amaze," Walter said, turning back to Phoenix. "When the whole city went dark on my way home the other night, I nearly fell out of the sky."

Lucy wondered if this was the same hawk she and Beckett had seen from the pier roof, flying north with empty talons. But when she tried to ask, nothing came out.

"Inexcusable of me to dump you and fly off that way," Walter went on. "It's been eating at me."

"Don't give it another thought," Phoenix said. "Without you I could never have gotten above that cornice. You were instrumental in saving our—their home."

As rats inside the pier caught the tenor of the conversation, some began to venture back out, though not very far.

"Glad to hear it," Walter said. "But when I think what that jet engine would have done to me . . ." A shudder rippled his feathers. "Anyway, I stopped by to offer you a lift."

"A lift?" Phoenix said.

"I owe my old mother another visit. I'd be more than happy to drop you in Manahawkin."

"What's Manahawkin?" Lucy asked, finally finding her voice.

"Where I'm from in New Jersey," Phoenix said.

"I'll take you right back to that pretty little pond," Walter offered. "Maybe that pretty little squirrel will still be there waiting for you."

Giselle! Phoenix hadn't thought of her in days. He wondered if she'd gone back to the pond from time to time to think about him. It didn't seem likely. She'd switched from Tyrone to him so easily, she would probably have switched to another squirrel by now. Though she *had* seemed to like him. *You have a wonderful tail,* she'd said. *In the sunlight you can see a little auburn in it.* Aware of the sun on his tail now, he glanced around at it and almost gagged. Giselle would take one look at him and run!

And yet, monstrous as he was, most of these rats were looking at him with admiration. Lucy especially.

"Don't go, Mr. Phoenix!" said the young rat who'd chased the foil ball.

This ignited an outcry against his leaving. When one rat shouted, "Phoenix forever!" it turned into a chant that would have gone on and on if Beckett hadn't opened his mouth again to speak.

"You know, Phoenix, you haven't done so badly here," Beckett said. "All those articles about you in the papers."

"Articles in the papers?" Walter said.

"And photos!" another rat cried. "Phoenix is famous!"

Hearing this ruffled Walter's feathers a bit, reminding him of his celebrity cousin. He squinted up at the sun and commented that it was almost noon.

"If I'm going to get all the way to Cape May today," he said, "I better be taking off. Want to come along, squirrel?"

As Phoenix glanced around, the wharf rats all shook their heads, silently coaxing him not to go—even Junior.

"Don't forget, Mrs. P. mixed up that pilatory for you," Lucy said. "I bet it'll bring your fur back."

"I was hoping you'd be staying with us at her place," Beckett said. "It's very spacious up there."

Lucy didn't add anything to this, but the look on her face was quite eloquent, and when the young rat who'd kicked the foil ball took hold of his tail, Phoenix felt himself surrendering.

"I appreciate the offer, Walter," he said, "but I think I'll stick around."

Rats applauded and high-fived as Lucy and Beckett beamed.

"I wouldn't have minded the company on the flight," the hawk said, "but suit yourself."

"Would I be overstepping to ask you a favor, Walter?" Phoenix asked.

"Of course not. You saved my life."

"Could I ask you one too, Beckett?"

"Name it," Beckett said. "You saved our home."

Phoenix scurried into the pier and fetched a scrap of paper and a pen from Lucy and Beckett's crate. When he got back outside, he asked Beckett to write something for him. Beckett took up the pen, and Phoenix dictated his note:

"Dear Mom and Dad, I wanted you to know I'm okay. I just relocated to Manhattan."

This was the one thing that was really bothering him about declining Walter's offer: the thought of his poor parents mourning his death. Walter and Mortimer looked on in amazement as Beckett scrawled the message on the piece of paper. "Relocated" and "Manhattan" were tricky, but he managed them.

"Anything else?" Beckett asked when he finished.

Phoenix nodded. "Maybe you could put: *I miss you. I'll try to visit someday. Love, Phoenix.*"

Other than leaving the *e* out of Phoenix's name, Beckett completed the note in style. "Can your parents read?" he asked, handing it over.

"Not that I know of," Phoenix said. But he had a feeling Great-Aunt Flo might be able to, since she'd taken the trouble to line her nest with newspaper rather than leaves. "You could find the pond where you snatched me, right?" he said, passing the note up to Walter.

"Of course," Walter said, taking it in his left talons.

"In the woods just north of it there's one white tree. A birch. Could you drop that at the foot of it?"

"With pleasure," Walter said.

Phoenix thanked him and offered to get him a nut or two for his trip.

"Nuts aren't really my thing," Walter said. "Though I don't mind the occasional rodent."

As Mortimer hit the deck again, the rats who'd ventured out fell over each other trying to get back into the pier.

"Just kidding," Walter said.

With that the hawk unfurled his mighty wings and flapped up into the sky. Mortimer got to his paws again, muttering under his breath. Most of the other rats edged back outside to catch the spectacle of the great bird's departure. As Walter flew out over the river, a flock of gulls following a charter boat squawked and cleared his path. Gradually the hawk gained altitude. When he veered south, Phoenix felt a pang of regret. But soon rats were crowding around him, and every time one of them clapped him on the back, it knocked a little more of the regret out of him.

Once Walter was completely out of sight, Augustus came rushing out of the pier with a plastic straw in one paw and a pebble in the other.

"I got a peashooter!" he cried. "Where's the bird?"

"As if you didn't know, you old charlatan," Mortimer said with a snicker.

Ignoring the comment, Augustus climbed onto the cleat and squinted left and right as if searching for his foe. "Looks like he skedaddled," he said. "Lucky for him. I guess we can get back to the business at hand."

By this he evidently meant the mayoral election. Beckett put up a struggle, but Phoenix and Lucy managed to push him onto the cleat again. The eldest elder was still too shaken up from his tumble to officiate, so the middle elder did the honors, directing those for

Augustus to his left and those for Beckett to his right. There wasn't a rat among them who'd failed to note the candidates' very different reactions to the hawk, and not even Helen and Junior hesitated to move to Beckett's side. As Augustus gaped at his totally empty section, the straw and pebble slipped from his paws.

Lucy and a bunch of other young rats pulled Beckett off the cleat and carried him into the pier at the place where the door was warped up. Most of the others followed, and as the rats' eyes adjusted to the interior dimness, a great majority of them saw their rundown home with a fresh fondness. They gathered around the steel drum, where Beckett had been set down. He'd had enough attention for one day and would have toddled off to his crate if there hadn't been so many expectant faces turned toward him. He looked to the elders for a hint.

"You might want to appoint new elders, Mr. Mayor," the youngest of them suggested.

"What's wrong with you three?" Beckett asked.

"Old Moberly appointed us," said the eldest, who was leaning on the middle one.

"Could I reappoint you?" Beckett asked.

"Certainly," the eldest said. "But you shouldn't feel you—"

"Great," Beckett said. "You'll do beautifully. Anything else?"

The elders were quite tickled. After another consultation the youngest said: "There's also the question of a sergeant at arms."

Rats looked around. As it happened, their former sergeant at arms was already halfway to Battery Park, but Augustus's wife and son were just inside the pier door. Helen had stopped Junior there to discuss their future. Forsaking their crate was a bitter prospect to her, but so was remaining on the pier as an object of pity after her spouse's disgrace. Though Junior didn't feel the humiliation quite as keenly as he did the bruises from his fall, he figured he had to stick by her, whatever her decision.

The two weren't far from the place where the pier door was warped up. A moment later Phoenix appeared there, rolling in the can of New Amsterdam ale. Mortimer, who'd talked him into pushing it the last leg, followed with Augustus's straw wrapped in his tail. "Hey, Phoenix!" Beckett called out. Phoenix eased the can to a stop.

"You're good-size," Beckett said. "How'd you like to be sergeant at arms?"

"Um, it should probably be a rat," Phoenix said.

Beckett looked to the elders again. "That *is* the tradition," said the eldest.

"Could he at least be a special advisor?" Beckett asked.

The elders raised no objection this, and when Phoenix didn't either, Beckett asked his advice about the sergeant-at-arms position.

"Lucy's strong," Phoenix pointed out.

"Oh, but I need her as my other special advisor," Beckett said.

Lucy smiled at this, quite sure her brother would dump most of the mayoral duties on her. "If you want my advice," she said, "how about Junior?"

"Yeah, he nearly made it up the substation," Phoenix agreed.

Junior went slack-jawed, and when Beckett beckoned him over, he was too stunned to move. They'd never exactly been pals. But his mother grabbed his paw and pulled him toward the others.

"Would you accept the appointment to sergeant at arms, Junior?" Beckett asked formally.

Helen wasted no time in pushing her son toward the new mayor. As she watched the two young rats shake on the deal, a terrible weight slid from her shoulders.

"Any other pressing duties?" Beckett asked the elders.

They couldn't think of any, and after all the drama of the last few days, it dawned on everyone that life could go back to normal. While Beckett made a beeline for his crate, Helen virtually floated up to hers, and those who'd packed up for the evacuation happily lugged their bundles back to theirs. The new sergeant at arms tried to talk the younger set into a swim. His soreness had miraculously disappeared.

"I can't wait to see you dive!" Emily cried.

"I can't do a really *high* dive," Junior said. "Come show us how it's done, Phoenix."

"Height's not as important as form," said Phoenix. "Your form is much better than mine."

The two locked eyes for a moment, and they both grinned. "Come on, Lulu," Junior said. "Let's all go."

But to Emily's relief, Lucy wanted to help Beckett move their beds to Mrs. P.'s. Phoenix offered to help Lucy carry her loafer, which was a good thing, since Beckett was totally preoccupied, agonizing over whether to bring a dog-eared *National Geographic* to their new digs. Mrs. P. was sound asleep and didn't even twitch as they maneuvered the shoe up the stirring stick. After they set it down upstairs, Phoenix had a chance to check the place out. Having grown up among majestic pines, he never would have believed he would choose to be stuck in a crate, but this upstairs apartment really didn't seem too bad.

They went back for Beckett's loafer. By the time they'd brought over Phoenix's nesting material, it was Phoenix's turn to worry about the half-eaten Babybel in Mrs. P.'s lap. But when he gave her a little shake, she opened her eyes with a smile and said, "You'll be wanting that pilatory, won't you? It's by the stove."

Phoenix fetched the thimble full of ointment from the infirmary.

"Rub it in all over before bed," Mrs. P. said.

"That's so nice of you," he said, eyeing the precious stuff.

"Nothing compared to what you've done for us, dearie."

After depositing the thimble by his nest upstairs, Phoenix came back down and followed Lucy to her old crate. Mortimer was lounging in his shoe. He'd opened the beer can and was sipping some out with Augustus's straw.

"Sorry you're all moving out," he said, sounding anything but sorry.

Lucy spent the rest of the afternoon helping Beckett sort through his reading material. Beckett wasn't a fast reader and knew perfectly well he would never be able to get to most of it, but he couldn't bear to part with anything that might prove interesting, so the stack for the fuel pile remained paltry. Meanwhile, Phoenix carried the Gruyère and the nuts over to their new place, where he decided to catch a little nap. But as soon as he lay down he felt antsy, and he soon got up and peeled the plastic top off his can of deluxe nuts. He popped two pecans, a walnut, two almonds, and a really big nut—a Brazil nut—into his mouth. But instead of starting to chew, he slipped down the stirring stick and out of the crate with the nuts in his cheeks. He surveyed the whole pier building and made his way over to the pile of wooden pallets. Some of the ratlings were playing near the steel drum. When none of them were looking his way, he crept under the bottom pallet and hid the nuts in a dark corner.

Soon he was back stuffing his cheeks with more nuts. He didn't even know why he wanted to hide them—though earlier, when Walter commented that it was almost noon, he *had* noticed that the sun was a bit off to the south, not directly overhead. Something told him that with fall coming he had to squirrel away food for the winter. Of course, he'd never experienced a fall or a winter, and it would have been far more convenient, and probably safer, to leave the nuts in the can. But that didn't keep him from spending the rest of the afternoon caching nuts in every conceivable nook, high or low, in the pier. He couldn't help himself.

He was hiding the last batch just as Lucy was carrying the meager pile of rejected reading material to the fuel pile, so he helped her and Beckett lug the rest over to their new place. Once they'd arranged Beckett's periodicals, Lucy suggested they all go to the roof to watch the sunset.

"You two go," Beckett said. "I need to read up on mayoring."

Even if Beckett had had a book or article on the subject, it was doubtful there was enough light left for him to read by, but he had a feeling they might prefer to watch the sunset by themselves. So Lucy and Phoenix tiptoed downstairs past Mrs. P., who was dozing with a smile on her snout, and out the door. Phoenix zipped up to the top of Mrs. P.'s former home and watched, impressed, as Lucy climbed up after him. But just as he was thinking she must have a little squirrel in her, she misjudged a crack between two slats in the second highest crate and slipped. She landed on a narrow ledge below and tumbled off it, bouncing all the way down and ending up flat on her back on the ground. A mother and two ratlings hustled over to see if she was all right, only just beating Phoenix, who got down the stack of crates faster than he'd ever climbed down anything. But before any of them could even offer Lucy a paw, she was getting up, laughing at herself.

"What a klutz!" she said.

"Are you really okay?" asked the mother rat. "That was quite a fall."

Lucy dusted herself off. "I'm fine, thanks. But how embarrassing!"

"It's steep," Phoenix said, cocking an eye back up the stack.

"Do you always climb down backward like that, Mr. Phoenix?" asked the bigger ratling.

Phoenix froze. He'd been so worried about Lucy, he hadn't even thought about his manner of descent. But Lucy's way of laughing at herself must have been contagious, for he suddenly burst out laughing himself.

"I'm afraid I do," he said. "I guess I've never been much of a tree squirrel."

"Unless I'm mistaken, you climbed *up* that substation twice," said the mother rat. "Now *that* took pluck. Nobody cares a straw how you climb *down*."

Both ratlings bobbed their heads in agreement. Lucy grinned and spanked the dust off her paws.

"This time I'll try not to make a fool of myself," she said, and she started up the crates again.

"Better stay right behind her, Mr. Phoenix," the bigger ratling whispered, "so you can catch her."

Phoenix did, but Lucy didn't need any catching. She made it onto the top of Mrs. P.'s old crate without another misstep. Not even pausing to catch her breath, she scampered up the yardstick. Phoenix dashed up right behind her.

Side by side on the pier's roof, the two of them took in the sunset. There wasn't a bird of prey in sight, though they heard the occasional squawk of a seagull and the whooshing sound of passing traffic helicopters. They also heard the gleeful cries of Junior and the rest, still at it down on the half-sunken dock. Farther out, the river was unusually tranquil, the silky water catching the sky's ambers and pinks. For a while neither of them spoke, but when the pinks began to turn to purple, Lucy said, "I bet I know what you're thinking about."

"What?" Phoenix asked.

"That pretty little squirrel by the pond where you're from."

"Actually, I was thinking how pretty this view is."

"But Phoenix, you've been high up in trees. And to the top of the substation. You've even flown with hawks. This must seem like nothing to you."

He had, he realized, seen some spectacular views, starting with that first time he slipped out of the nest and climbed to the top of his parents' pine. But when she asked what the most beautiful view was he'd ever seen, he didn't have to think long.

"This," he said.

"Really?" she said, wide-eyed. "Why?"

"I guess . . . it must be the time of day."

It *was* a magical time of day. But again he may have been fudging a bit, for the best views are always the ones you share with someone—though just then he probably would have found a storm sewer beautiful. The river was almost as calm as the pond where he'd been snatched, so he could imagine looking off the end of the pier and seeing himself in the water, but with the pier safe and his downward climbing no longer weighing on him, not even the thought of his reflection could darken his mood.

"It must be the time of day" seemed to satisfy Lucy, however, for she inched sideways until, mangy as he was, they were actually touching. Then her stomach growled.

"I'm so sorry!" she cried, mortified.

"Are you hungry?" he asked.

"Well, a little, I guess," she admitted.

Phoenix went off to a corner of the roof, lifted up a piece of loose tarpaper, and pulled out a nut. He'd stashed three up here earlier but took only one back to Lucy. It was pale and round.

"I thought we ate all these!" she exclaimed.

"I found this last one in the bottom of the can."

"Why'd you bring it up here?"

"It's a squirrel thing," he said with a shrug.

Smiling, she insisted they split the nut, so he stuck it between his impressive front teeth, bit down very gently, and spat out two perfect halves. When he handed her one, she held it up.

"To home," she said, and she popped the half nut into her mouth, not minding in the least that it had been in his.

Phoenix echoed the sentiment, tapping the roof with his furless tail as he savored the snack.

Acknowledgments

For her encouragement and astute reading of the first draft of this novel, my heartfelt thanks go to my wonderful agent, Holly McGhee. For the look of the book, I owe a huge debt to the talented Greg Stadnyk, and of course to Gabriel Evans, who miraculously channeled these New York/New Jersey critters from his home on the other side of the world. As for my brilliant editor, Caitlyn Dlouhy—she not only helped shape this book in countless ways, she bestowed its title. Finally, I'd like to acknowledge my deep gratitude to the late Gregory Falls, who instilled in me a love of storytelling before I could even read.